Divergent

Also by
John D. Lambert
Coming Soon in the Intersections Romance Series

Chrysalis
Toast
Resonance

Where love meets life's unexpected paths.

This tender series of short Christian romances celebrates normatively divergent hearts—intersex, neurodivergent, and beautifully unique—finding gentle, grace-filled connection with another. Each story weaves positive Christian faith into journeys of acceptance, healing, and love that honor God's diverse design.

Available Now

Crimson Leaves: Poetry Celebrating Romance

Bask in the glow of love with *Crimson Leaves*, where every page whispers the language of romance.

Celebrate romance with the finest ancient, old, and contemporary love poetry from great poets worldwide, featuring:

- Over 200 love poems, timeless and new
- Heartfelt quotations and meditations
- Passionate letters and lyrics
- And introducing Poetic Hugs & Kisses™

Divergent

Book 1 in the
Intersections Romance Series

JOHN D. LAMBERT

RESOURCE *Publications* • Eugene, Oregon

DIVERGENT

Resource Publications
An Imprint of Wipf and Stock Publishers
199 W. 8th Ave., Suite 3
Eugene, OR 97401

www.wipfandstock.com

PAPERBACK ISBN: 979-8-3852-7291-4
HARDCOVER ISBN: 979-8-3852-7292-1
EBOOK ISBN: 979-8-3852-7293-8

Contents

Divergent: Departing or deviating from a norm, standard, or expected pattern.

Divergent Person: Someone whose thinking, behavior, aptitude, or body consistently resists fitting into a single dominant category, faction, or pattern—especially in systems designed to enforce conformity.

Preface

Divergent HAS TWO CHARACTERS who each have unique divergent traits among many possible traits, and what is depicted in these characters should not be generalized to other people.

Of *Divergent's* two protagonists, one is on the autism spectrum (ASD Level 1)—a divergent mind—and one is intersex—a divergent body. Both medical conditions can have symptoms that vary widely among all people with the same condition, so these two characters are just two examples of how their conditions can develop.

For instance, the medical condition of this intersex character usually leans male, and most individuals with this condition live fully as men.

Yet a minority with the same condition develop more female-leaning traits than is typical for that diagnosis. This story follows one such individual.

Most people are biologically male or female, but not everyone. A small percentage are intersex— having reproductive or sexual anatomy that doesn't fit typical definitions of exclusively male or female.

Many different conditions can cause someone to be intersex, and each condition (or combination of conditions) can produce a wide range of physical traits.

Some of these traits are obvious at birth (especially ambiguous genitalia), some become apparent only later in life, and some are so subtle the person never notices them.

Pitches

"Mr. Stanford's coming up," an executive assistant announced to the small group in the executive boardroom.

They ignored the expansive view of New York City behind them as the men straightened their ties and the ladies smoothed their skirts just inside the ornate mahogany doors.

"This guy better be worth all this," one muttered.

"Shirley's done her homework," replied Colton Wingate, an IT expert and billionaire board member, frowning at the complainer. "Stanford's a genius, but reclusive. We're lucky he's here."

Shirley added, "Mr. Stanford's a world-class prodigy, and after a famous success with his last company, he's looking for something to keep himself busy.

"However, he's peculiar in several ways and his social skills may not be what we're used to. Remember it's not his social skills we'd be contracting him for, so let's not offend him. Especially you, Walter."

A couple of minutes later the doors swung open and Olivia Masters, another IT expert, brought Stanford in and began the introductions.

"Mark, this is Walter Meade, CEO of Pilot Star Holdings, which controls our flagship company Pilot Star Hospitality. Mr. Meade, this is Mark Stanford, formerly Chief of User Experience at Quantum Foresight."

"Welcome, Mr. Stanford," Walter said, his tone guarded. "We're eager for this discussion."

"Thank you, Walter. It's an honor to meet you. Please call me Mark. I've read a lot about you recently."

During each introduction, Mark used his carefully researched and practiced routine of focusing his attention solely on that person, varying his compliments, and using the same grip strength the other person used. He also cupped his left hand on the outside of the handshake, and repeated each of their names at least once when he responded to them.

After all the official introductions, the hosts began to move toward their seats, but Mark didn't. Having spotted two people on the sidelines he hadn't been introduced to, he walked over and introduced himself, first to the stenographer for this meeting, and then to an executive assistant.

Walter scowled and the other executives exchanged curious glances, but the stenographer and executive assistant gazed at Mark in pleasant surprise.

All the executives other than Walter were smiling again as Mark was ushered to his seat at the table, across from all ten executives arrayed on the far side.

Mark didn't sit immediately, and said, "It feels a little adversarial this way. Would two of you mind sitting next to me to make it a friendlier ambience?"

Walter scowled, but waved a hand. "Half of you move."

"Actually," Mark replied, "I'd prefer just one on each side of me so I can still see everyone easily. If there's more than one, the nearest person would block my view of the others."

Everyone turned to look at Walter, who waved again. "Do it. Let's get on with this."

As the other two men sat down next to Mark, Walter rapped his knuckles on the table and growled, "I don't care who you are, Mr. Stanford, if you try another power play, this meeting's over."

Mark hesitated as he blinked rapidly a few times and cocked his head very slightly. "I… I don't know how to do corporate power plays. Or how to recognize them. I apologize if I inadvertently committed one, or more than one."

Walter sniffed. "Shirley?"

"Mark," Shirley said with a warm smile, "you've seen our Request For Proposal for a new guest app for Pilot Star Hospitality, but you've only had it three weeks because we only recently found out you might be available.

"Since our proposal deadline is in two weeks and the big consulting companies have had it almost three months, this meeting is to try to level the playing field for you by cutting down on the numerous back and forth information requests and replies."

When she stopped speaking and gazed at him expectantly, he said, "Thank you…

"I've had your RFP two weeks and three days, but I'm ready to submit my proposal today. I just wanted to explain it first."

Many of the executives shot questioning looks around the room as Walter's face darkened.

Not seeing the expressions of concern, Mark continued.

"Your current guest app is hated, and you know it, which is why you're willing to spend millions of dollars over the next two years—hoping your new app won't become a new example of failed IT consulting contracts wasting tens of millions of dollars and years of time, and speeding up your decline in market share and tanking your stock.

"My proposal's to deliver an app in a maximum of 31 weeks, which your guests will love, because it will be designed from the guests' perspective, not yours, which is why I rewrote your requirements, while keeping all the features specified in your RFP."

Murmurs rippled through the room, but Mark didn't notice.

"How good will your new app be? You won't have to wait the two years specified in your RFP to find out. You'll know within a few weeks.

"I'll give a demonstration once a week, starting the second week, and show my working app to Shirley and anyone else you want. After the first demo, each week I'll highlight how I've improved it from the prior week.

"You won't be looking at a mockup or prototype that may or may not work someday, you'll be looking at something that's working as you look at it. You'll be able to put it on your own smartphones and actually start using it.

"After four weeks, if you don't like my work to date, I'll leave and you won't ever pay me a cent. But you also won't get to keep any of my code or system design.

"If you like it, I'll keep going on the app and help your IT team prep the scale-up for the public launch, and in no more than thirty-one weeks from the start of my contract, your already tested and proven app will be released to the public."

Mark went on, explaining his compensation requirements, which were just as unorthodox as everything else, and most of it would be based on stock gains, if—and only if—the company's stock rose beyond a significant threshold within one year after the public rollout of the new app.

"This way," Mark said, "if the app doesn't help your stock improve significantly, my stock terms will be worth nothing. But if the gains are very large, I'll earn more than any of the consulting companies are likely to charge you.

"Please bear in mind, however, that if this pays off for me, for every dollar I gain, PS Hospitality gains far more. And if you go with a contractor who delivers another app guests hate, your stock will tank.

"After the rollout," he continued, "I'll be happy to stay on for a while to manage future app changes, since apps always need new features or to adapt to changes. Eventually, I'll hand it off to your IT to maintain."

Then he explained enough of his system design to wow the IT experts in the room.

"Next," he said, "my proposal also includes a draft contract. It has a few easily completed placeholders, but it's very atypical compared to a project managed by a Fortune 500 consulting company. My contract is fourteen pages in total."

Mark glanced at the executive lawyer present.

"The way it eliminates hundreds of pages of legal boilerplate and hidden terms where lawyers on both sides fight over how to better protect their side, is by replacing extensive details with a handful of operating principles and… trust. Actual human-to-human trust, but with principle-based guarantees and insurance.

"You can ask any of my former colleagues about my character, and if we act with trust and integrity, we can avoid the kinds of failures that end up in court, which is what those extremely detailed contracts are for.

"Plus, I've written the contract so it actually gives you protection superior to my own since it's integrated with you reviewing a working design each week.

"After the first four weeks, you can pull the plug at any time prior to public launch if you don't like the app I'm making. If you do, you'll owe me nothing else and you can resume your process of choosing a major consulting firm, losing only a few months at most.

"However, if you hire me, based on my proposal and draft contract, you eliminate bureaucracy, you can see actual production-ready progress week by week, you can have all your RFP-specified features live in a maximum of thirty-one weeks, and I'm staking my primary financial reward on my certainty that your market cap will grow by more than ten percent within twelve months after that."

He took out his phone and tapped a button as he said, "I just sent my proposal to the submission address and to Shirley, who can further distribute it."

Then he slipped the phone back into his jacket.

"Any questions?"

There was a bit of an uproar for a few minutes, during which Mark didn't respond at all.

Some of the folks were hostile, some defended Mark, and some stayed out of the fray.

Only after Walter demanded order did Mark begin replying to one person at a time, sometimes providing more detail, but often a question only needed him to repeat what he'd already explained.

After that had been going on a while, an arm reached around Mark and placed a drink close to him with a note reading, "Already thoroughly shaken."

Mark instantly recognized his favorite brand and type of protein drink, which he normally had at that time of day, and he glanced back to see that it had been the executive assistant Todd who had provided it.

A little later, Walter told Mark he'd like the company to have a discussion without him, and Mark got up to leave.

Todd approached to escort him elsewhere to wait, and Mark turned to ask Walter, "Is it alright if I wait in a private area, and is it okay if Todd keeps me company there?"

Walter grunted, "Yeah, yeah," and gave a wave as both approval and dismissal.

As soon as the door closed to the small conference room, Mark casually asked, "Who told you what I like to drink?"

Todd smiled. "Oh, no one, sir. I didn't know anything about you when I heard you were coming today, so I did a quick crash course on everything I could find out about you in the time I had available.

"That included how important it is to your routine and health regimen to have your mid-morning protein drink."

"Thank you. I really appreciate that, but please remember to call me Mark. And, I'm curious… how many did you buy?"

Todd grinned. "Four. Just in case. And they have a long shelf life in case you return."

"Todd… would you mind giving me your career plans in a thirty-second elevator pitch?"

"Oh? Um, okay... Mark. They call me an executive assistant, but I'm really just a gofer in a suit.

"I don't have what it takes inside to be a cutthroat businessman, and I wouldn't want to. I want to be good at what I'm doing now unless and until I come across something I can do better.

"I'm not very ambitious, if that's what you were expecting."

"Well, first," Mark replied, "it annoys me when I hear someone say they're *just* something, as if that's all they are, so don't ever do that again.

"You're not *just* a gofer. You're a marvelous person full of promise... and you're also excellent at your current job. The initiative, ability, and effort you put into researching me is proof.

"Now... I estimate low odds of them giving me this contract because my proposal is too unconventional. But if they do give it to me, I'll need a personal assistant, since my last one needed to move due to her husband's job.

"Do you want the job? I'll pay you twice what you're earning now for a minimum of one year, give you twice the paid time off, and I'll give you one percent of whatever I earn from this contract—including from the stock."

Todd stared in disbelief.

"Are... are you joking?"

"I don't know how to joke," Mark said.

"Oh, yeah, I read that. Well, it'd be stupid to turn down an offer like that, sir—I mean Mark. So, yes, thank you!"

"Good," Mark said, then took a deep breath and let it out. "Oh, wait. I should warn you I have few social skills, despite my mother drilling me on them from childhood until I left for college.

"Well, I've also added a few based on my own study and practice, but if you're my assistant, you'll see my social weaknesses frequently. Do you want to reconsider?"

"No, Mark, not at all."

"Okay, then. And if I end up somewhere else, might you be willing and able to move, if I paid for it?"

"Y-yeah, absolutely!"

"Let me put your name and contact info in my phone. I may not be working here, but I'm going to work somewhere. I'll check with you when I land and see if it's somewhere you want to go."

Work

After what Todd learned was a knock-down-drag-out fight in the board room, it was tentatively agreed to accept Mark's proposal if it passed legal review and the full board of directors approved the stock part of the deal.

To the surprise of many, it did, two weeks later, and with a caveat added by Mark for Todd to be his personal assistant.

* * *

Three weeks after the contract was signed, after the second weekly app demonstration, Todd commented to Mark, "That went extremely well."

"Yes," Mark agreed. "Next week they'll be even happier, which should predispose them heavily toward invoking the clause to have me finish it, which also triggers you working directly for me."

Todd was beaming as they navigated the rest of the way back to Mark's office and his own outer desk.

He didn't expect his duties to change, but his compensation sure would—as long as nothing went wrong. As long as he didn't somehow disappoint Mark—as he almost had the first time he'd started to tidy up Mark's office mid-day.

Mark didn't get angry, but he did get upset, and from then on, he always straightened up after Mark was done for the day.

Meetings between the two of them were usually very short, so Todd usually stood, but this time, back in his office, Mark gestured for Todd to sit on the only other chair in the room.

"My previous assistant was adequate, but you're excellent, Todd—far better than my high expectations. You keep surprising me at how well you anticipate my needs, you're excellent at gatekeeping for me, you do high quality research quickly, and you've been learning fundamental principles of user interface design, resulting in you making excellent UI suggestions."

Todd stared wide-eyed until he became self-conscious of it and forced himself to stop, although he couldn't suppress a blush.

Mark continued, "It's my perception that you're a very introspective person, so I said all that in case you have any doubts about why I want you to keep working for me and to dispel any notion you might have about me reneging on the compensation I originally promised.

"However, I'll need to add to your duties once the four-week transition occurs and you become my employee.

"My last assistant was an employee of the same company I worked for, and I've never had an employee, so I'll rely on you to find attorneys, accountants, and whoever else you need to consult so you can set up payroll and benefits for yourself.

"My phone has an entry under Lawyer and another under Accountant, so you can start with them, with the idea that if what we need for this isn't in their skillset, they can refer you to other people who're suitable."

As soon as Mark had said, "I'll need to add to your duties…" Todd had gotten out his smartphone to start taking notes.

"I'd also like you to monitor the company's compliance with their token payments to me of $30,000 a month so I don't have to distract myself with that.

"By the way, I can honor my financial commitment to you regardless of whether I get any stock benefits from this company, or I would've made the commitment conditional.

"I exercised all my stock options and cashed out of the last company I was at, invested all of it in certain blue chip stocks, and my cost of living is much lower than the dividends I'm earning now."

Todd was amazed at how open Mark was being with his personal information, and wondered if that was normal for wealthy people to share that kind of information with their personal assistants. But then—it was Mark, so being normal wasn't normal.

Mark was gazing up and off to one side, as he often did when deep in thought, and Todd took the opportunity to speak up.

"I took some finance and accounting courses for my business degree."

Instantly, he regretted making an unimportant comment and disrupting Mark's chain of thought, and hoped it wouldn't make Mark mad for the first time.

Mark slowly turned to look at Todd… and smiled. "That's good to know… and that makes me wonder what else there is about you I could know but don't.

"And, come to think of it, it might help you to know more about me…."

Mark thought for a moment again, and there was no way Todd was going to interrupt this time.

"Get me a copy of your résumé, please. And your college transcript. Get yourself a copy of my résumé off my phone and order my transcript from MIT.

"My rationale is that the more we know about each other, the better we'll be able to work together, taking both our strengths and weaknesses into account."

Todd blushed deeply as he reached out to take Mark's phone off his desk.

"Please don't power it up in here. There'll be a lot of notifications as soon as you do, and I don't want to hear the chimes."

"I could turn the chimes off for you," Todd offered.

"No, I need to be able to… hey… wait a second… you're already managing my email… how would you feel about keeping my phone during the day and checking notifications for me? In case there's something urgent."

Todd had no more than started to nod and Mark considered it settled.

"At first, you'll have to guess about what I consider urgent enough to be interrupted, but you'll learn quickly.

"Oh, there're sometimes media requests for interviews. Go over those with me at the end of each day when they come in, and you can reply the next day.

"And I think that's all for me for now. Do you have anything?"

"No, nothing right now," Todd said as he rose, feeling both exhilaration at new challenges and fear at the possibility of failing at things he'd never done before.

At the door, Todd added, "I'll do my best for you, Mark."

"I know. You already are."

* * *

With the executives loving the design and the rapid progress, and the corporate IT staff loving their interactions with Mark and Todd, the company exercised its right to have Mark stay on after the first four weeks.

Then a wrinkle cropped up.

Todd entered Mark's office with more excitement than usual and closed the door to wait for Mark to get to a breaking point.

"Colton Wingate's on the phone," Todd said quickly the moment Mark looked up.

"Oh. Huh. Okay, put him through. Then come back in."

Todd hurried out and transferred the call.

"Hello, Colton," Mark said when he answered.

"Please hold for Mr. Wingate," a voice said.

"Mark, this is Colton Wingate," he said moments later. "My representative at your weekly demos tells me you have no intention of acting on our suggestions for the app. Is that true?"

"No," Mark replied, "we're keeping track of all suggestions and requests and will let Shirley's team prioritize them for implementation—with my guidance. But that will all happen after the rollout of the app based on the original RFP requirements."

"That's unacceptable," Colton said. "My guy's suggestions should've been in the RFP because they need to be in the app when it first rolls out. Make it happen."

Mark blinked rapidly and furrowed his brow, then asked, "Do you know how common it is for projects to be ruined by scope-creep requests? Would you allow someone to unilaterally change the terms of a contract you were working under?"

Colton huffed. "These are important changes, Mark. Critical."

"Then your rep should argue for them being at the top of the priority list for changes when that time comes, but—"

Colton interrupted, "We can execute a contract modification and extension if that's what you want. That's fine. But this needs to happen.

"And you owe me this—you wouldn't have this contract if I hadn't pushed hard for you, with both the committee and the board."

When Mark didn't reply quickly enough, Colton asked, "Okay? Are we agreed?"

"No," Mark replied. "That might be normal for most people, but that will be more disruptive than I can handle. I won't be able to maintain my focus on the system design and coding—mostly coding at this point.

"It would change the framework I'm working under, and set a precedent that the framework could be changed any number of times. That uncertainty won't merely cause me a slight delay, it will destroy my ability to work."

Seconds ticked by.

Then Colton cursed and the line went dead.

"He hung up on me," Mark said to Todd, then told him Colton's side of the conversation as he carefully reviewed it all for his own sake.

"Have you dealt with a situation like this before?" Todd asked.

"Mm… employer demands beyond my abilities, yes, but not quite like this, and not from such a strong personality. I wish I could've not made him angry, but under the circumstances, I think it was unavoidable."

"Do you think he'll cause trouble?"

Mark considered that a moment, then replied, "I have no idea. If he wants to, he might be able to convince the company to terminate my contract, which I would find very disappointing, but at least I could live with that. If I tried to do what he's asking me to…"

Mark shivered, and gazed toward the ceiling.

"Well," Todd said, "I'll be your assistant as long as you want me—here, or anywhere else. Including while you're hunting for another job or contract, if you want me."

Mark slowly turned toward Todd, slowly relaxed, and slowly smiled.

"I'd like that very much, Todd. I appreciate that a lot right now."

* * *

For the next few months, Mark focused on coding, and made rapid progress—and Todd's assistance gave Mark the long uninterrupted hours he needed.

Late each afternoon, Todd would stay to restore order to Mark's office after he'd gone.

As those weeks rolled by, every week all the PS Hospitality staff at Mark's app demonstrations were very happy, although Colton Wingate's rep was usually frosty.

Throughout it all, Todd dutifully added suggestions and requests to a long and steadily growing list.

At twenty-four weeks, Mark was wrapping up all the original requirements and announced the initial contract would be fulfilled at twenty-five weeks.

On the Thursday afternoon of week twenty-four, Todd opened the door to Mark's office, entered, closed the door, and quietly waited—as he often did.

Moments later Mark got to a good place to pause in his work and looked up at Todd.

Unlike Todd's normal behavior, this time he hesitated before speaking, and when he did, his voice wavered.

"I, uh... I was wondering... if maybe we could have a little celebration..."

"Hey, that sounds nice, Todd. What did you have in mind?"

"I know you never go to parties, but, well, I can cook decently. If you'd like to come over to dinner tomorrow night at, say, seven, we could have a quiet dinner together? I know pretty well what you like to eat and drink and what you don't."

"That would be very nice, Todd. Thank you very much. Oh, wait..."

Mark thought while Todd worried.

"I need your help about the time. You said seven o'clock, but I probably can't arrive at exactly seven, so what do people normally do?

"They don't get there early and then stand outside waiting to ring the doorbell right on the dot, do they?"

Todd sighed with relief and suppressed a grin. "You're right, they don't. People usually arrive within a window of time either a little before or after, and ring the bell and go in as soon as they get there.

"Except my apartment doesn't have a bell, so you'll have to knock."

Todd noticed Mark concentrating, and thought to add, "Oh, and for most people, I think a little before or after typically means up to ten minutes before and up to twenty minutes after..."

Mark's expression switched to a smile.

"People often show up later than that," Todd said, "but I think they start to be regarded as bad guests if they do—unless they have a good excuse, and don't make it a habit."

"Perfect," Mark said. "Oh, and I'll need your address. I've never been there before."

"It's already on your phone in my contact info, Mark."

"Oh, yeah? Okay, tomorrow at seven. And please remind me right before we leave the office tomorrow."

Dinner

At eight minutes before seven o'clock, Mark knocked sharply on Todd's apartment door.

A few seconds later, a lock clicked and the door swung open to a smiling hostess.

"Welcome, Mark, please come in. I'm Samantha Wells, and you can call me Samantha, or Sam, if you prefer. I know a lot about you from Todd."

Mark didn't move, other than his eyes widening and his jaw going slack.

Concern began to rise on Samantha's face until Mark could manage to start talking.

"Uh… um… Todd… didn't tell me… that you… that, uh…"

Samantha's smile returned to its full glory and she waved for him to enter as she said, "Oh, right! Well, I hope you don't mind if I join you for dinner."

"Really? Uh, no. I mean—I don't mind. I think. I mean… I mean—I'd like that very much…"

"Then why don't you come inside?" Samantha asked as she gestured again.

This time, Mark entered, and Samantha closed the door.

"May I take your coat?" she asked.

"Coat? My… oh! Okay… yes," he said as he started taking it off, then paused. "Uh, Todd didn't say to dress formally. I, uh—"

"Oh, no, it's not formal at all," Samantha assured him. "What you're wearing is fine. It's excellent."

He stared as she hung up his coat, then she took his arm and led him the few steps into a modest but very orderly living room.

"I hope you like the way I look," Samantha said after letting go of his arm and taking a step back.

A bit of worry crossed her brow. "You keep staring at me. Is something wrong?"

Mark gave a twitch of surprise. "Wrong? Oh, no! Far from it! I just… you're so beautiful… and my social skills are very poor in certain unfamiliar situations… like this…"

Samantha's concern didn't lessen. "Are you teasing me, Mark?"

"Oh, no, Ma'am! I, uh, don't know how to tease. And I doubt I would if I could. I sincerely think—oh, wait! Are you Todd's wife? I didn't— he never—"

"No, silly. You should know Todd's not married."

"Then you must be his girlfriend."

"No, he doesn't have a girlfriend right now."

"Sister?"

Samantha giggled, the worry mostly gone. "No, but—"

"Are you married or engaged to or dating someone besides Todd?"

Samantha blinked, then blushed as she held up her left hand to show her bare ring finger. "Uh, no, I'm not… I'm… single…"

Mark gave his head a quick shake. "I'm confused. I don't understand how a woman as beautiful and as nice as you is single."

She drew in a sharp breath.

She took a step closer, and gazed into his eyes.

"Do… do you really think I'm beautiful? Really…? Truly?"

"Samantha, you're the most beautiful woman I've ever seen."

She stood still a long moment, then she closed the distance between them. She put her hands on his chest and whispered, "And you're the most handsome man I've ever seen…

"Please...

"May I kiss you?"

Mark stammered again and started breathing faster. "I— I, uh, d-don't know how..."

Samantha rose up on her toes and leaned into him as she took Mark's hands and placed them on her hips.

"Lean your head down, tilt your head a little to your right, close your eyes, and then we'll gently press our lips together."

Mark followed the instructions and felt her lips touch his, and his eyes popped wide open, but he quickly closed them again to adhere to the protocol.

It made an even bigger impression when he felt her lips part slightly, and then he started making a few muffled sounds, but without taking his mouth away from hers.

Then he felt her tongue touching his lips and he started squirming along with the noises, yet he still didn't pull away his mouth or his hands. Then she pushed her tongue into his mouth slightly, and he started trembling and shaking, and finally broke the kiss.

"That... that..." he panted, "was overwhelming."

"I'm glad you liked it as much as I did," Samantha whispered.

Mark appeared dazed and wobbly. "Literally overwhelming... I may... pass out..."

"Oh! Quickly, sit down, Mark! Lean back, and catch your breath. I know you almost took mine away."

Mark sat, but instead of leaning straight back, he turned to lean back against the arm of the sofa. "I apologize, but I think... I—"

He passed out, and Samantha panicked, not knowing whether to try to wake him up or let him rest.

She rushed to bring a glass of water and put it on the coffee table, deciding to wait and see if he came to quickly, which he did. Sort of.

His eyes opened into slits and he barely whispered, "If I die, it was worth it…"

"Oh, no, Mark, don't talk like that! Well, not the first part! Do you really think it was worth it, though?"

"I could seriously die happy, right now, Samantha," he panted as his eyes returned to normal. "Thank you for giving me the first kiss I've ever had, and such a wondrous kiss… would you mind… could I impose… to ask you to kiss me again?"

Samantha hesitated. "Would that knock you out again?"

Mark thought a moment, then replied, "Now that I know what to expect, I suspect I'll be able to handle it better. I sure would like to try."

Samantha got on her knees beside the sofa, leaned over, and gently kissed him.

This time, he only moaned quietly behind the kiss. They continued to kiss as Mark's hands found their way to her hips again without her help. When his hands started to drift up toward her breasts, she took hold to stop them, and then she broke the kiss.

"My body's tingling all over," Mark said. "Is that supposed to happen?"

"I don't really know," Samantha replied. "That was only my second kiss, too."

Mark's eyebrows went up. "Am I dreaming? You're too good to be true."

Samantha got off her knees and sat on the edge of the coffee table, trying to think of a reply. She started fighting tears, and the effort added to her frustration.

"I don't want to cry," she quietly moaned. "I don't know what it will do to my makeup."

"Why might you cry?" Mark asked. "What did I do wrong?"

She dabbed at the first tears. "You didn't do anything wrong, Mark… I did…"

Samantha started crying hard, quickly getting up to grab a box of tissues off the end table and using them to try to protect her makeup, but then sitting back down on the coffee table next to Mark. Mark slowly eased up into a sitting position.

"You haven't said anything," Samantha said when Mark still didn't reply.

"I haven't the faintest idea of what to say or do. And I haven't the faintest idea of anything you might have done wrong."

Samantha's crying got worse again, and when she could talk again, she started with a deep breath.

"I tricked you. I'm sorry, but... I've been so desperate... I never planned to kiss you. I'd planned a little speech for right after you came in, but...

"The way you looked at me...

"The way you flattered me...

"I forgot everything I'd planned..."

Mark's face was scrunched up as he was trying to interpret what Samantha was saying, but making no progress.

"I'm Todd," Samantha finally said.

Mark's face changed to a different kind of puzzlement. Finally, Mark was the first to speak again.

"Oh, I'm not very good at discerning humor. Or satire. Especially satire. But I think this is humor, right? A joke?"

He glanced around the rest of the apartment and called out, "Okay, Todd, you can come out now."

Samantha's face was tortured. "Mark... it's not a joke... I really am Todd. I— I—"

"Now, Samantha, there are many things I don't understand, but I know you're a woman and Todd's a man, so I can't deduce why you're persisting with this ruse. Or why Todd is still hiding."

Samantha sighed and cried as she gazed at his face. "Mark... an hour ago I put on a dress, a wig, and makeup. Right before you got here, I put on high heels. I was an idiot, and I didn't realize how unkind it would be to fool you like this, and, and… I'm sorry. I'm so sorry I did this."

Mark pondered, then said, "I don't see how it's possible for someone who looks like Todd to look like you. And even if the physical appearance could be believed, you don't sound like Todd."

She dropped her chin and eyes.

"My voice has always been kind of high compared to most men, as if I never went through puberty, but my voice changes when I put on clothes like these.

"I didn't even have to learn how, it just happened automatically. My voice becomes higher-pitched, and softer, somehow. And I can't control it. I can't turn off the voice change without changing back into male clothes."

Mark started to say something, but Samantha beat him to it. "*Please* don't ask me to change clothes right now. It would break my heart. I put so much into trying to look as pretty as I could for you, and your reaction was so far beyond what I'd dared hope for… just… please don't ask me to prove things to you that way."

Mark sighed. "Okay, Samantha. Or Todd. My mind is only marginally functional right now—compared to when I'm like I usually am, I mean, I think, considering that my mind always has major shortcomings—but how about this? I'll try to come up with one or more questions for you that only Todd is likely to be able to answer."

Samantha gave a solemn nod, still softly crying.

"Now, obviously, Todd could've told another person anything he knows, so you might be able to answer any single question if Todd thought to mention it to you, no matter how esoteric. So, that's why I'll try to pick several questions, each of which is highly unlikely for you to know, unless… unless you really are Todd in addition to Samantha."

He shook his head, then sighed again, then closed his eyes to concentrate while Samantha waited.

"Okay," Mark finally said, "first question. What was the very last thing I said to Todd before arriving here tonight?"

Samantha let out a breath and smiled, the tears stemmed for the time being. "You said, 'See you then,' and before that you said, 'This better not be a blind date thing,' and I had to suppress a laugh and said 'I promise it's not a blind date.'

"And that was true because I think a blind date is someone you haven't met before, and you've known Todd very well for six months now—sorry, twenty-four weeks. Then I said, 'Remember, it's at seven o'clock,' and that's when you said, 'See you then.' "

While Mark was thinking, Samantha added, "And I suppressed a laugh because as Todd I never laugh because it comes out as a very girlish giggle, which I've always hated, except recently, as Samantha. So… I know you've never, ever heard Todd laugh."

Mark slowly narrowed his eyes, folded his arms across his chest, and tilted his head as he gazed at her, then he finally straightened up again.

"Okay… when was the last time I told Todd he did a good job?"

"Never. Not once. You've always said, 'Excellent work,' and you say it frequently, multiple times a week, and the last time was yesterday after I finally got Dr. Timken on the phone for you."

Mark's head tilted forward ever so slightly as his jaw went slack, and he blinked several times. He shook his head hard, then gazed at Samantha again.

"About three months ago," Mark said, "I left the office a while and I brought Todd back a sandwich. Where was it from?"

"Deniyon's. I remember because you go out so infrequently, so it stuck in my mind. And you laughed about it when I told you they'd wrapped it up in four layers of paper wrapping."

Mark's jaw dropped and his mouth fell open. Then he shook his head again.

Dichotomy

"You have to be Todd... but you can't be Todd."

"Mark... I'm so sorry... but I *am* Todd. I'm so sorry I deceived you this way. I thought it was a good idea but I was extremely wrong, and I'm sorry. Please... please don't hate me..."

Mark waved a hand to dismiss the notion. "I'll never hate Todd or Samantha. But... I don't know if my mind will ever be able to reconcile this strange dichotomy."

They were both quiet for a while until Mark asked, "So Todd was the original, and discovered somehow he could put on a female disguise, and wanted to test its effectiveness on me because he trusted me to keep it confidential?"

"No. Well, I never thought of that, but maybe that's true for part of it. Maybe that was in the back of my mind..."

"Do you mind telling me what was in the front of your mind?"

Samantha closed her eyes a moment, then got up and sat on the far end of the sofa and stared at the floor in front of her.

"You know the difference between XX and XY genes?"

"Yes."

"Well, I have XXY. Do you happen to be familiar with that?"

"Only that it exists, along with some other variations. I've never studied it."

"Well, I've studied it because I have it. It's called Klinefelter syndrome... which only happens to male babies.

"I— I even tried praying a few times when I was young, begging God to fix me, to make me normal, but nothing improved… so… I just kept going. Just doing the best I could. Until… until I met you."

"Anyway, they estimate a large percentage of baby boys with it don't survive past birth, and those who do survive are around one in 500 to 1,000, although it could be somewhat more common if there are a lot of undiagnosed cases…"

She took a couple of deep breaths.

"It can cause a wide variety of problems… like it's probably why I have a body shape that's more feminine than masculine. And my voice. And it's probably why I never had any sexual desire…

"Many KS boys are taller than average, but obviously, I wasn't one of those. I'm only five-foot-one-inch tall. Most also tend to have pudgy stomachs, and that's why I eat very little, to make sure I don't get fat."

"In high school I thought I was sexually attracted to women, but I never tried dating…

"I was diagnosed as a toddler, but when I turned fifteen I was tested and confirmed infertile… I didn't think that would matter anyway, because no girl would want me due to… my other XXY symptoms.

"In college I figured out I wasn't sexually attracted to women—or men—and what I'd always felt about women was simple admiration of their physical beauty. And that's the way I expected the rest of my life to be… until a few months ago."

Mark felt sympathetic, but Samantha was still staring blankly at the floor.

"That's when I met you. Well, before we met, I studied you after I was told I'd be the assistant at a company meeting that included you.

"You know it's my habit to learn everything I can about someone to accommodate them as well as possible while they're at a meeting I'm supporting. So, before we even met, I had a lot of empathy for your uncommon traits.

"Then, the day we met, your extraordinary kindness was obvious to everyone as introductions were made.

"The executives had never introduced me or a stenographer to a guest before, but you all but ignored the executives a few minutes while you introduced yourself to me and the stenographer on duty that day.

"And you treated us with just as much courtesy and respect as you gave the executives.

"They brought you in because your programming and design skills are the best in the world, but your kindness and consideration for others is equally world class in my opinion. And that's why… that's why I fell in love with you."

Mark was astonished, and had trouble following a moment as Samantha continued.

"It took me months to figure it out, but now I know I fell in love with you that first day we met. And I'll bet there are lots of women, and some men, who share that experience. You're truly unique. And desirable."

Mark interrupted. "But I'm not romantically suitable for anyone. I guess I'm fertile, but I'm certain I'd be a terrible husband and a worse father, and I wouldn't want to risk inflicting that on anyone. That's why I never bothered studying social skills relevant to romance and marriage…

"I go from one work-related hyperfixation to another, ignoring everything—and everyone—else. That's been effective for my career, but it makes it impossible for me to be an adequate romantic partner."

Samantha replied quietly while still gazing at the floor. "No, you're wrong about that.

"Even when you're generally fixated on work, you have a natural and extreme empathy and consideration for others, even to the point of caring more about others than yourself.

"By the way, I think that's part of what makes you uniquely able to design app interfaces that users love right from the start."

"Well," Mark said, "I wasn't considerate enough to refrain from interrupting. You were explaining what led to tonight, and that you fell in love with me, but I don't understand how that led to… Samantha."

"Ah. Well, for the first few months of me working for you, I was really struggling internally. My life had been satisfactory and steady, and all of a sudden, my emotions were in turmoil, and I couldn't understand what was going on.

"My understanding evolved… painfully slowly… and once I finally began to realize I was in love with you, that made no sense. It was impossible.

"We were both guys. And I'd learned from bits and pieces of conversations with you that you're attracted to women and women only.

"Then… then I got the crazy notion to wonder if *I* could appeal to you as a woman…

"I actually questioned my sanity because of that, but I couldn't stop thinking about it, and the more I thought about it, the more it made sense in my warped thinking…

"My body has a lot of feminine characteristics. I'd tried hard to ignore those all my life, but the idea popped into my head… what if I stopped ignoring them? Suppose I did the opposite, and tried to harness them?

"Suppose… I tried to develop a purely feminine persona?

"That got me scared that if I did try, it might be dangerous, so I looked it up—and there are things like that which are out of the control of the people who have them, but I thought my new persona would be in my control, like an actor playing a role in a movie, so it'd be safe…

"So I started experimenting, alone, here, with clothes, make-up, wigs, prostheses, and high heels—"

"Oh!" Mark exclaimed. "Breast prostheses! That solves one of my riddles! Oh, sorry again. Go on..."

After giggling nervously a moment, Samantha continued, still staring at the floor, "I chose the name Samantha Wells just because I liked it...

"And as I experimented, I seemed to be having success after success, and each success got me more excited, although I didn't think about why. And I didn't think about how I might go from dress-up to the appealing-to-you part, but I kept pushing forward, and getting more emotional, and I'd never been very emotional...

"And at some point I started thinking... XXY genes affect everyone differently, and in my case... despite having severely underdeveloped male bits on the outside, I had more feminine traits overall than masculine ones.

"So... I thought... maybe... maybe I should have been Samantha all along.

"Then a few weeks ago, a realization hit me hard. Your initial contract was coming to an end. I knew you already had a follow-on contract, but... what if something went wrong with that?

"What if you left the company and if... if you didn't take me with you wherever you went next?

"I wanted to rationally rule that out, but being rational wasn't an option. My emotions were in full control.

"I became desperate, and for weeks I didn't even fully know what I was desperate *about*. Then I finally figured out I was desperate not to lose you.

"I already knew I loved you, without you ever knowing, even though we've been working closely together. And for a while, I thought if that ever ended, I'd just love you from afar.

"But when the desperation hit... I realized I don't just love you, I need you. I need to be close to you. I need your friendship. Your companionship. I need everything about you in my life..."

"And... with that in the background, and since I'd been playing dress up so effectively, I instinctively and impulsively invited you to this private celebration dinner so I could show you… that I can do what I thought was a pretty good job of being feminine.

"And foolishly, I— I didn't think past that. Maybe fear kept me from thinking about what might happen after I showed you Samantha.

"And just this second I realized what an idiot I've been not to face the difference between appearing feminine and being female."

Samantha sighed heavily. "I guess I've ruined our relationship—the very thing I was so frantic to save."

They were both quiet, and Samantha still couldn't bear even a glance toward Mark.

Finally, Mark broke the silence.

"Your ability to appear feminine is truly exceptional, Samantha. I've never wanted to kiss a girl as much as I wanted to kiss you. And I've never had more than a pale desire to have sex… until I kissed you.

"I think… no… I'm sure… for your sake, I'd have thrown away my private plan to never date or marry. Except…"

"Except I'm not a woman, and you're heterosexual," Samantha finished for him.

They were quiet again until Mark asked, "Are you heterosexual or homosexual, Samantha?"

She took a very deep breath, and turned her head completely away from Mark.

"My body isn't completely male or female, so… what would hetero or homosexual mean to me?

"Although it never mattered because I was asexual in the sense that I had no serious sexual desire for anyone, and even if I did, I wouldn't be able to perform.

"But all of a sudden recently, I guess I've become mixed up emotionally in addition to biologically.

"I want to be a normal female so I can have sex with you, but I have male reproductive organs. They're very small—even for

XXY… and except for peeing and a very tiny amount of testosterone production, they're non-functional, but they're there. I'm sorry."

Again, they were both quiet, and Samantha started quietly crying again, wondering if she'd spend the rest of her life reliving this night that had gone so horribly wrong.

And once again, it was Mark who broke the silence.

"I had no idea of the struggle you've been going through, Samantha. I'm sorry I wasn't able to be supportive through all that, and I'll have to learn how to be supportive in the future…

"And Samantha… you've changed me… something deep inside. First when I saw you… my reaction was unique for me. And then when you kissed me.

"Something changed, and I don't want to ever go back to what I was before. I don't know if I could even if I wanted to, but I don't want to.

"I hope you don't doubt my sincerity or seriousness, but I want you to know I want us to have a future together for the rest of our lives, whatever that might turn out to be."

Now it was Samantha who was astonished, and she didn't even breathe for a moment as Mark's last statement sank in.

"I would never have considered going to another company without you, Samantha, and I still won't. I never will.

"Not because of the work you do, because I could hire someone else for that, even though I doubt anyone else would be half as good…

"But because… whoever you are… whatever you are… I love you."

Samantha flinched at the words, and froze in mid-nose wipe. Then she quickly turned her head around to gaze at Mark.

"I love you," he repeated. "If I'm not too old for you, I—"

"You're only four years older than me!" Samantha blurted, then thought to add, "That means no, you're not too old for me!"

After her second statement, Mark seemed greatly relieved.

"Then… Samantha… I want you. Somehow, some way. Every way. I— I've never wanted anything more in my life."

"I'm a mess," Samantha cried plaintively. "My makeup is probably ruined and I don't look pretty anymore and my emotions are shot and all my stupid brain can think about is how much I want to kiss you again right now…"

"Really…? You'd be willing to kiss me again?"

"Willing?!"

She half jumped up before launching herself into his arms and smothering him with kisses.

Union

Mark twisted to lie back on the arm of the sofa again, pulling Samantha on top of him, kissing the whole time.

When gasping for air forced their mouths apart, Mark panted, "My body's on fire… I'm burning all over… It's some kind of crazy… extreme… something."

Samantha pushed herself up a bit. "Do you need to stop? Are you going to pass out? Should I get off you?"

"Even if… I pass out… I don't want you to get off me…"

"Mark, I have… maybe I'm crazy, but… I have an overwhelming desire for sex with you right now. If I was a woman… I'd be ripping your clothes off, but I… I don't know what to do…"

"You don't have a vagina…" Mark said, considering it out loud. "So if we want sex, I think the remaining options are manual, oral, or anal… do you want to do any of those…?"

"There're also silicone panties with an artificial vagina," she said with excitement, but immediately lost it all. "But I don't have any…"

"Oh?" Mark replied. "Well, we can wait."

Samantha furrowed her brow. "Bear in mind, I'm not thinking this out rationally, I'm just telling you what I feel right now…

"I think I'm sexually aroused, and I've never felt like this before. But right now… I really want to make you feel good.

"I want to do everything that makes you feel good, but only what makes you feel good. And I don't want you to try to make me feel good physically.

"That part of me doesn't work, and I only want to use my body to make you feel good, if that's possible."

"That would make you subservient instead of equal—"

"I'm not equal. I don't want to be equal. I want to make you feel good. That's the only thing that will make me feel good emotionally, which is all I'm capable of… to know I'm making you feel good…"

"That doesn't sound right to me."

"Maybe you've been too conditioned. Forget popular opinions about relationships and listen to me telling you want *I* want. What *I* need. I need to make you feel good. That's everything I need. So please, let me serve you without you serving me. Okay?"

"I don't like that, but… that's what you want me to try to do?"

"Yes!" she said as she started unbuckling his belt.

As Samantha continued, Mark's brain shifted from fully lucid into a semi-rational state, little more than a passenger in his body.

Sometime later they got to a point where Mark needed a break. He was bare from the waist down, but she was still fully dressed as she rose enough to unbutton Mark's dress shirt and pull it open.

Then she stood, and Mark's eyes slowly turned to gaze at her in a stupor.

"I can't believe I'm doing this," Samantha whispered. "I can't believe I like this. But I love it. I feel like I was born for this… for you. I love touching you intimately. I love making you feel good…"

She smiled as she reached behind her back and unzipped her dress, and Mark's eyes went wide as she slowly pulled it off her shoulders, then lowered it to the floor, revealing lacy purple underclothes.

She tried to burn Mark's intense look of desire into her memory.

"Do I please you like this?" she asked.

Mark licked his lips, swallowed hard, and blinked.

"I've never been able to get physically aroused..." she confided, "so at least I don't have to be embarrassed or humiliated by that. My body's never made enough testosterone or other androgens for things like that."

Mark could only blink.

A little while later, Samantha lightly rested her upper body on his and they felt each other's breaths rising and falling.

"I love you, Mark. Whatever may come, I love you."

Mark managed to move one arm to put a hand close enough to stroke her hair as he whispered, "I love you, Samantha. Will you spend the rest of your life with me?"

Samantha gasped.

"Mark... maybe you're just caught up in passion right now. After you've had more time to think—"

"Samantha, are you afraid I'll change my mind at some point? Because that won't happen. Sometimes I'm very decisive, like when I asked you to work for me.

"Recognizing my desire for you now is one of those times, and I'm certain already that it isn't something that will ever change in me."

Samantha's expression mixed hope with doubt as Mark continued.

"I once wondered if I was aromantic or very mildly romantic, or some other odd variant.

"When I studied that briefly, I read about borearomantic—derived from Boreas, the Greek god of the north wind, which implies a rare, unique gust of wind...

"And now I know that applies to me. Now I know what romantic attraction is. For me... it's you. It's only you. It will only ever be you.

"I fervently hope this won't scare you away, but I want to spend every day and every night with you. I want to grow old with you.

"You're the only person that's ever been true for, and there will never be anyone else. You and you alone are perfect for me. Please say you'll be mine forever."

"Oh, yes, Mark, yes, my love!" she bawled. "No matter what!"

When her joyful crying subsided, he said, "I'll never leave you, Samantha, and I'll always take care of you to the best of my ability."

After they caressed while repeating vows to each other and rested a while, Samantha asked, "Shall I get up now?"

"No, not yet, if you don't mind," Mark replied. "I really like this. I can feel your heartbeat. And you smell nice. Can we stay like this while we talk?"

"Sure! Just let me adjust a little. And—ouch—let me say that I know your fixations better than anyone, and I can be happy serving you without you needing to interrupt your focus..."

Moments later she was comfortably nestled against him as his fingers toyed with her hair and he took a deep breath.

"I think I've mostly come back to my senses... and if you want to, I think you could keep working in the office as Todd, and be Samantha at night—if it doesn't bother you to switch that frequently.

"However... I don't fully trust myself not to slip up—like if I absent-mindedly call you Samantha at work. Or... instead of that...

"Todd could resign immediately or as soon as you want to, then, after a few days, I could hire Samantha as my new assistant."

"Hmm," Samantha responded. "I'd like to table making a decision on that and discuss another topic first. How would you feel about me getting surgically altered and taking prescriptions to help make my body more feminine?"

"I'm opposed. If that's what you want, or if you have reasons you think that's important, I'll do my best to consider them with an open mind, but I fell in love with you the way you are now. I wouldn't want to risk your health in any way by trying to change your body."

"That's a loving perspective, Mark. Thank you. But do you know what options are available?"

"No, not a clue. I just tried to start with a principle that could encompass everything."

"I know, and maybe that's the best way to start as a default—and I *love* your logical mind—but I'd like to quickly go through a list of the biggest options and see if you might feel differently about any of them."

"Sure," Mark agreed. "Now?"

"Yeah. I'm loving right now, too, but I'm also eager to go over these. By the way, I insist you have veto power over everything. Now first… I could get my little penis and tiny testicles removed."

"Veto. I hate that idea. Removing your testicles would alter your hormones. Removing your penis wouldn't do anything worthwhile and might cause future complications."

Samantha nodded with a smile. "Okay, then I think leaving those would rule out me getting an artificial vagina made from a length of my colon…"

"Oh, heavens no. Countless things could go wrong with that. If you don't want the other methods of having sex, we can go back to not having sex.

"As long as we can still hug and kiss, I think I can be content."

"Well, based on the last half hour or so, I really love the methods we've already used—and how you react to them."

"Tonight is the only experience I've ever had," Mark replied, "and I'm very grateful for what you've already given me."

Samantha sighed contentedly. "Prescriptions to change my hormones? That's out, based on what you said before?"

"Yes. Fiddling around with hormones is extremely risky, and the whole interconnected system has so many untestable feedback loops that can't be isolated, I have no confidence that research into them will ever be fully or accurately predictive."

"Really? I thought taking hormone supplements was supposed to be no big deal."

"On the contrary, I studied hormones when I wanted to know if they might help me, and ended up taking vitamins D3 and K2 with magnesium as a result. D3 is both a vitamin and a hormone.

"But among many other things, I learned that even the moderate doses of estrogens in birth control pills can cause serious problems like blood clots or wreck someone's mood for years.

"And the huge doses given to actually change sex traits are an order of magnitude more dangerous."

Samantha's eyes widened as Mark continued.

"Hormones are one of the fundamental ways different parts of the body send signals to each other, and the complexity is beyond human comprehension.

"There are at least 10,000 distinct biofeedback mechanisms—all the way down to the molecular level.

"That alone defies our understanding, but virtually every one of those feedback loops interacts with other feedback loops."

"Wow," Samantha said, and then was quiet for a long moment before continuing.

"Well, okay then. That issue's settled…

"What if I stop being Todd, and let my hair grow out and stop using a wig?"

"Oh. Okay, I have no objection to that. In fact, I might like that very much. I'm glad you wanted to go through this list with me."

"Yay! Thank you! And… how would you feel about me getting electrolysis to permanently remove my facial hair?

"I don't have much, but I'd like to get rid of what there is. It's not a dangerous process at all, and lots of women with a little bit of facial hair have that done…"

"Okay, then. That sounds reasonable."

Samantha took a deep breath and let it out slowly. "Do you feel like... like breast implants would be useless and needlessly dangerous?"

Mark didn't reply right away.

"What's wrong?" Samantha asked. "I know that look. You're not just thinking, you have something to say but you're hesitant to say it."

"Well... you're right... I hesitated because you didn't raise that issue like you raised the others, and you seem... more tense about it.

"Are you afraid I'll ask you to get them?"

Samantha grinned and kissed his chest. "No, Mark, my love. It's the opposite... if we decide I'll stop being Todd, I'd like to get them.

"I'd be happy to get them for your sake even if I didn't want them, but the fact is I do want them. I think... they'd help. Plus, my emotions want me to, and my brain is abstaining from the vote."

Mark chuckled at her vote comment, then got serious again. "Do other women ever get breast implants for themselves—not just to please their husbands?"

"I think that happens frequently," Samantha replied. "I think quite a few women who have small breasts do it if they can afford it, and most women who have their natural breasts removed due to cancer like to get implants to feel more normal.

"I think I feel kind of like flat chested women, and maybe a little like women who had mastectomies, even though I never had big breasts in the first place."

"Well," Mark replied, "that seems like it might be minimal risk for surgery. Um... I hate to impose, but um... if you get implants... could they not be too big? Not huge?"

Samantha smiled. "What's huge from your perspective, Mark?"

He cupped his free hand way out from his chest and Samantha giggled loudly.

"I agree with you, Mark, those would be huge. And much, much bigger than what I was thinking…

"My breasts are actually B-cup size. Ever since they started growing shortly after puberty, I've worn a compression band and loose shirts to hide them.

"One of my doctors suggested breast reduction surgery, but they quit growing, and at this size I decided I was okay with the way I was already hiding them.

"Despite their size, though, and my large nipples, their shape doesn't look like natural female breasts. The last couple of months… as Samantha… I've come to think wearing a compression band every day for many years has permanently distorted my breast shape, and that's why I've been testing breast prostheses.

"The kind I'm wearing now correct my shape, but… if I'm wearing them anyway… I've decided I have a preference for a C or D cup size. These prostheses I'm wearing are C-cup. With implants, I think this or a D would be a modest increase in size, while giving me a natural-looking shape."

"Hmm…" Mark said. "Well… we could talk to a leading plastic surgeon and see what they have to say about the dangers, and if we both think it sounds safe enough, then I'll agree."

"Great!" Samantha said with another quick kiss to his chest. "In that case, I want to stop being Todd!"

"Samantha… if it means that much to you, why didn't you say so to start with?"

"I didn't want to pressure you into agreeing to something you might otherwise be opposed to. This way, we're both happy…"

She raised up a bit. "Now, would you like me to make you feel good again, or do you want dinner now? It'll take me five minutes to finish it and put it on the table—correction, my love… *about* five minutes."

Mark smiled at her effort to phrase things in ways that his brain preferred, the same as he'd quickly come to appreciate in the office months ago.

"Well, if you don't mind, I'd like it if you did something to me again first, and then a quick shower, and then dinner."

"That sounds perfect," Samantha agreed as she began.

Mark moaned and said, "Samantha, so far I haven't played an active role—I've been too overstimulated—but I think I've been acclimating rapidly. After dinner, I'd like to take you to bed, and I'd like to take the lead."

"I'd love that!"

"And... maybe after you've gotten some of those panties with a silicone vagina... I might want to try being... forceful. But only some of the time, and not dangerously so."

"Oh, I'd really love that! And... I'm hoping we'll spend the night together?"

"Tonight and every night."

"Um... *every*... night?" Samantha muttered.

Mark looked puzzled. "I'd like us to spend every night together from now on. Have I misinterpreted something?"

Samantha gave her head a quick shake. "No, I... I guess that just caught me off guard.

"I want that too, but this is so sudden, I think it's going to take me some time for all this to really sink in."

"Yes..." Mark agreed between moans. "Everything this evening has been sudden to me, too."

When they were done, Samantha got up and started cleaning them both up, and Mark asked, "Is your shower big enough for both of us at the same time?"

Samantha froze in panic.

"Mark... I can't shower without reverting to Todd. Would you mind waiting to shower together until my hair has grown out and I've gotten breast implants? And I'd like to always wear panties or something in front of you, and a bra until I get my implants."

"Sure, Samantha. That will give me more time to enjoy anticipating our first shower together.

"And don't think I didn't notice you implied that getting implants is already a firm decision."

"Oh, I don't know," Samantha replied. "I was thinking I'd get soft ones instead of firm ones."

She paused, then added, "That was a pun, Mark."

"Ah. It doesn't bother you that you have to explain things like that to me?"

"On the contrary, when it happens at work, it makes me feel useful to you, and I love that. And I like it here at home just as much.

"But speaking of work again," she went on, "at work, I'll serve you the same as I always have. And at home, I can keep you company, I can cook, keep our home clean, and give you sex as often as you need or want it.

"And by the way, I'm guessing you tend to be as disorganized at your home as you do at the office, so I expect it's a mess."

"A huge mess, Samantha. Messes. Everywhere."

"That's okay. It makes me feel good to get and keep things organized for you."

"Then my apartment should make you feel great."

"Mark, was that a joke?"

"Not intentionally. On a related note, your apartment now has huge sentimental value to us, but mine's almost an hour closer to the office."

"And in your apartment building," Samantha said, "yours is probably much bigger than mine."

"I could be perfectly happy here, Samantha, as far as apartment size goes. But I think during all those extra hours of commuting, I might regret us not being able to spend that time alone together.

"And I just mean being alone with you, regardless of what we're doing. Like at the office, where you keep people without appointments away from me."

Samantha embraced him, they kissed a moment, and then just hugged as her hands roamed up and down his back.

"I can picture us old and gray," Mark said, "sitting in front of a fireplace, with you gazing into the fire and me gazing at your beauty."

"Mark... that's very romantic, and I love it. I know you well, but I didn't know you had that in you."

"I think that just developed tonight. Thanks to you being bold enough to be Samantha, and breaking through my shell. That was extraordinarily brave, and we have our new romantic relationship only because of that."

Samantha sighed dreamily, then snapped out of it and broke their hug.

"I'm looking forward to lots more of this, but right now I've got a man who needs a shower before a great dinner that you're going to love!"

She gave him a gentle shove toward her bathroom and started to rush to her kitchenette, but stopped herself.

"Oh! Okay, I'm going to the bathroom with you so I can use the mirror before you get it fogged up. *Then* I'll get dinner on the table!"

Unconventional

Samantha's mostly waterproof makeup choices had held up surprisingly well, and Mark loved her cooking.

After eating and admiring each other across the table for a while, Mark smiled and said, "You're too good to be true… in a figurative sense, of course. You're perfect for me… is it merely a coincidence that we met?

"Rationally, that seems plausible, but… irrationally… it feels impossible that it's coincidence. I can't imagine my life without you."

Samantha put her fork down. "Soulmates. I think we're soulmates. I never thought about destiny before, but I sure feel it now."

They ate a bit more and Mark said, "Let's discuss what we're going to tell our families."

"Oh! Oh my, I never considered that! Oh… I'll need some time to think about that."

"Take all the time you need, but it seems to me if you stop being Todd, you're going to have to tell them something sometime."

Samantha winced. "Yeah, that sounds right… but it also sounds terrifying. I'm an only child, so it's just my parents, though."

Mark swallowed a bite, then replied, "What about uncles, aunts, cousins, and grandparents?"

Samantha's mood dropped. "Oh… yeah…"

Mark paused, then asked, "Your parents knew about your XXY chromosomes all along, right? Have they always been supportive?"

"Oh, very supportive, always. My parents noticed a variety of very early developmental problems like delayed coordination and speech, and learning disabilities. That led to testing that found my XXY genes."

"Did your parents know about how you developed after puberty?"

Samantha blushed deeply, and spoke quietly.

"Yes, for the most part, and I think they hurt more than I did, all along. I think they might have felt like it was their fault. But they were always loving and supportive."

"Were they good male and female role models?"

"Oh, yes, absolutely. The best."

Mark smiled. "Then we can predict with confidence that they'll support you changing to Samantha. And you could let your mother tell your extended family."

Samantha thought for a second, then her face lit up, and a moment later she jumped up to go around the dinette table to Mark.

He quickly stood up and she hugged him tightly, burying her face against him.

He stroked her hair and said, "I suggest you call them soon and tell them on the phone rather than going back as Todd and telling them in person, and then switching to Samantha, which might seem a little abrupt…

"Once you've explained over the phone how you decided to experiment, and how it seemed more natural to you, I'm equally confident they'll not only be supportive, but they'll be happy for you that you've found a life that's better than what you had before."

"Then… then I could go see them as Samantha…"

Mark kissed her head. "Yes. And you could send them a photo of Samantha before you go—or before we go—to help set their expectations."

Samantha gazed into Mark's eyes. "You won't mind going with me?"

"I'd mind not going with you."

Samantha sobbed a moment, but that quickly faded and she said, "They already know all about you—not about us, but about you…"

She looked up through watery eyes and smiled. "I bragged about working for you. And I bragged a lot."

After Samantha was calm enough for them to resume their meal, she asked, "What about your family, Mark?"

"If you have no objection," he replied, "I'll text them all and tell them I have a big announcement, and schedule a video call.

"Then we'll call them together with you and me sitting side by side, and I'll introduce you as Samantha, tell them I met you at work, we fell in love, I just asked you to marry me, you said yes, and we didn't wait, so we're already married."

"If you don't mind, I want to put it that way because my heart already belongs to you and to you alone, and you've indicated you feel the same way toward me. Everything else is just decor…

"By the way," Mark continued with a perplexed look, "how often do married couples have sex?"

Samantha grinned. "There's not a standard schedule, Mark. We can do it as often or as infrequent as you want. But… clarify something for me, please… in your mind… we're already married?"

"Yes. We can have a small, private, formal wedding later, if you'd like, and we can get a family lawyer to do whatever needs to be done to change your legal identity and whatever else might need doing…

"But yes, in my mind, we just got married, you are and always will be Samantha, and our honeymoon started about an hour ago."

Samantha's face showed a combination of delight and puzzlement. "That's... I... really...?"

"Perhaps I should elaborate," Mark said. "You've said you already loved me before I arrived tonight. The moment you opened the door, my usually dormant emotions woke up.

"When you told me you weren't married, engaged, or dating, I wanted you.

"When you asked to kiss me, and I said I didn't know how, you explained it to me in a way I could understand and follow, and that's when I fell in love with you.

"When I later asked if you would be willing to kiss me again, you jumped into my arms and kissed me. At that moment, it became an absolute to me. I belong to you, and you belong to me, forever. I think that's the moment we became married.

"And our honeymoon began a few minutes later, followed by a very informal wedding when you agreed to spend the rest of your life with me."

Samantha was grinning again. "You *really* don't care much about what's conventional, do you?"

"I care about things like being reasonable, efficient, and honest, whether those result in things that are conventional or not. Does that bother you?"

"Oh, no! That's part of what I love about you! And on an evening when my highest hope was that you would still like me after showing you Samantha, and when I thought I ruined everything... you completely turned it around.

"But also flipped it upside down... at least for me.

"The idea that we've just gotten married is... *so* unconventional. That's something else that's going to take me time to wrap my head around."

"We can still have a conventional wedding, Samantha," Mark said. "As big and formal or as small and intimate as you want—but my preference is for small, if you don't mind too much.

"And whenever you want, you can start planning a trip for us to visit your parents and mine as a remote-working vacation.

"Oh, and you'll need an engagement ring, and we'll both need wedding bands. How's all that sound?"

"Far beyond my dreams, Mark. Far beyond."

"Not too far, I hope."

"Well..." she mused out loud, "how would you feel about something like this?

"How about if I leave most of my things here for now, and each weekend I come here alone to sort and pack and bring one box back to your place each Saturday and one each Sunday?

"We'd be spending every night together, but I'd have some alone time here to help me adjust my mind to my new life."

"Oh. Okay. Yes, happy times can be just as emotionally stressful as hard times—even though they're more pleasant—and we need healthy ways to cope with it. You think that kind of time alone will help you do that?"

"I hope so... I think if I don't try to hurry, the easy physical activity would give me time to think, and help me get used to so many changes.

"I'd like to try that."

"Physical activity and reflection are both healthy coping mechanisms," Mark said. "But do you think that will be enough?"

"Possibly... but I think me spending time organizing your apartment will help, too—once I get past the shock of however bad your messes are."

"Um... maybe we should just hire a company to strip my apartment bare and just start from scratch."

Samantha giggled. Mark didn't.

* * *

Three very busy weeks later—and one week after their civil wedding at the City Clerk's Office—Mark emerged from his office for his mid-morning stretch and protein shake.

Samantha was grinning as she handed him the drink, which she'd already shaken.

"You got an email from the CFO acknowledging that the stock closed yesterday just over ten percent higher than the official pre-app stock price, triggering your major stock benefits."

"You told me about it meeting the requirement yesterday after the market closed," Mark said, "but it's nice that they've officially acknowledged it."

"And EuroLux Hospitality Group called again to request a meeting with you… and Shirley scheduled extra time for your next app demo because they want to have a party. And Colton Wingate's going to be there."

"Ah. I hope he's not still mad at me. I added half the things he wanted urgently in the first two weeks after rollout, and I'll have the rest done by the end of the day tomorrow. That's under the thirty-one weeks I'd set as my maximum time limit just for the original requirements."

Samantha reassured him, "I don't see how he could still be upset since the stock market is reacting this well and him owning so much of it.

"Oh, and I didn't like him mistreating you on the phone, so I've been spending a little time studying him. And… I noticed he increased his stake in PS Hospitality by almost twenty percent the first day of the insider trading window. So he should be extra happy thanks to you."

"Well," Mark replied, "thanks to himself, too, for helping me get this job. But during the party after the demo, I'd appreciate it if you'd stick right beside me."

"I know, Mark. I'll be there."

He paused, then started walking back into his office as he said, "I feel safer when I know you're with me. Emotionally safer."

He didn't notice Samantha—still at her desk—as her face lit up, her chin came up, and her shoulders went back.

The location of the next app demonstration was moved to a much larger room than normal, and it was still crowded.

Shirley talked about how their ad campaign featuring happy app users had two videos that had gone mildly viral, and social media reactions to the app were overwhelmingly positive. Reservations were surging at every hotel in their portfolio, and the stock price trend was still going up.

Then she introduced Mark to enthusiastic applause, Mark gave a quick review of the main feature groups, and then demonstrated the features added in the past week. He concluded to wild applause, and the noise level made him wince.

That was followed by a reception, which tested Mark's social endurance. As it was winding down, Colton Wingate asked Mark to follow him to a private room, and was irritated that Mark insisted on Samantha staying with him.

Samantha was concerned about how much Colton would drain Mark's social battery, and what might happen if it went dry before this impromptu meeting was over.

"I've heard a competitor's hoping to recruit you to rewrite their guest app," Colton said as soon as the door shut. "If that's true, you need to understand that your stock deal here makes it in your financial interest not to help our competitors."

"Three of them are," Mark replied, "but whether or not that would be in my financial interest would depend on how much they offered versus my potential stock increases here—with and without my making an app for a competitor."

Colton looked angry, but only until Mark added, "But I've long ruled that out for another reason."

"Oh?" Colton said. "What reason?"

"It would be a conflict of interest. You may have had someone check my contract and noted that it doesn't prohibit me from writing a competing app... but my integrity does. I consider that an unwritten obligation."

"Well... good," Colton replied. "Make sure you remember that. And you still owe me a favor for playing an instrumental role in you getting this contract."

"No," Mark said, and Samantha hid a smile. "I repaid that debt by successfully fulfilling the contract and thereby increasing your wealth—along with my own and that of every other stockholder."

Then Samantha could no longer contain her pride and beamed at Mark's defending himself against someone who didn't seem to be used to people saying no..

Colton huffed. "All right, Mark, I concede that. But I'm considering buying a stake in another company that might benefit from your skillset. What are the chances you'd consider that for me?"

"I'd be honored to consider it, Colton, if I'm available at the time. And we're already in the process of identifying the team that will take over maintenance here, and I'll start training them after I get back from a road trip."

"Good to know... thanks," Colton said. "Now I've got to get out of here. Again, great work on the app, Mark, and it was a pleasure to meet you, Mrs. Stanford."

"It was a pleasure to meet you, too, Mr. Wingate."

* * *

"Got your earplugs and sleeping mask handy?" Samantha asked the next Friday morning.

"Yes," Mark confirmed, as he leaned back in the rental car's passenger seat and put the mask on. "And my weighted blanket is packed in the trunk.

"I'll leave my earplugs out for now. If there are no sirens or jackhammers or horns honking or... on second thought, I'll put them in now.

"Once we get out of town and in a steady flow of highway traffic, tap me, and I'll take the earplugs out, and the drone of the engine, transmission, tires, and wind flow should be okay."

"That sounds good, Mark."

Several hours later they were in Samantha's home town and she pulled into a shopping center and parked.

Mark pulled up his eye mask, glanced around, and looked quizzically at her.

"Mom and Dad's neighborhood is just up ahead," she said. "And if I'm going to follow the adage not to drive when you're too emotional… I need you to drive now, if you're up to it. Otherwise, we—"

"Yes, I can handle it. As long as you don't mind me driving very slowly."

"Thanks, Mark."

Mark thought things over as they got out to stretch and trade places, and as soon as Samantha got back in, she texted her mom that they were only a couple of minutes away.

"Samantha," Mark said, "you know your mom's happy about this and your dad's come around to it… so… are you just excited, or are you nervous?"

"Both. Mostly nervous, though. Momma said his back was acting up, and he might not be able to come out to greet us when we get there…

"That's what they've always done before—seeing me off, and watching for me and coming outside together when I've come home to visit. I'm scared maybe Dad hasn't accepted my change as well as Momma's implied."

"Ah. Do you want to wait, or—"

"No, let's go, please. Turn right out of here, and I'll tell you turn by turn. It's not far."

"Okay, but tell me turns way ahead of time, please."

It took a lot more than a couple of minutes with Mark driving, but when he pulled into the driveway, both Mr. and Mrs. Yates were outside, with her father using a four-leg walker.

They greeted Samantha enthusiastically, then Samantha introduced Mark, and he was reassured by how similar the event was to his own past visits to his parents.

After they'd all sat and talked for a long while, Samantha went with her mom to help in the kitchen, leaving the two men in the small living room.

"Don't worry," Mr. Yates told Mark, "you don't have to talk. I don't understand your issues any better than I understand… Samantha's… but… you make… *her*… happier than I've ever seen… *her*… before, and that… that's more important than anything else."

Mark drummed his fingers, then asked, "Is this a suitable time for me to bring in our luggage?"

"Sure, yeah. Your room's the first door on the left."

Mark gave a small nod, went to the front door, and paused. "There are lots of things Samantha and I don't understand about ourselves, either. But we love each other."

After dinner, the girls cleaned up while Mark and Mr. Yates went back into the living room.

The men were quiet a few minutes, and then Mr. Yates said, "I taught… Samantha… to ride a bicycle… right out there on that sidewalk.

"I didn't spend enough time with… her… growing up, but these days I spend a lot of time remembering the times we did spend together."

Then he told more stories about Samantha, and when Samantha and her mother joined them, Mrs. Yates told a story about Samantha. Then another.

Samantha excused herself, went to her old room, and returned with a wrapped gift.

Mr. Yates was in his recliner because it was easier on his back, and Mark put a dining chair beside him for Mrs. Yates so they could open the present together.

Inside were two 8 x 10 pictures in identical frames—one was the very last picture of Todd, taken in the corporate office, and the other the very first picture of Samantha, in her old apartment.

Mrs. Yates jumped up to hug Samantha as tears streamed down her face, and Mr. Yates' eyes watered.

"This was all Mark's idea," Samantha said. "Taking both photos in the first place, and then getting framed copies for you."

"Oh, this is so wonderful, Samantha! Thank you so much, Mark! Oh… but we need a picture of both of you together!"

"You've got some of those on your phone, Momma. But we can get one of those framed for you, too. Maybe for your Christmas present?"

The farewell was even more emotional than the reunion for Samantha and her mother, and while they were hugging and saying their goodbyes next to the car, Mark stood quietly beside Mr. Yates and his walker.

"Mark," Mr. Yates said, "Those two pictures you gave us… both of them… we… I… I can't tell you how much those mean to us."

"I thought if I was in your situation, that's what I would have wanted," Mark replied. "That, and for me to take care of Samantha to the best of my ability."

"Well, son… you've made a fine start."

A week after that, Mark and Samantha flew out for a Stanford family get together, and Samantha was the belle of the ball—the extraordinary woman who had captured Mark's heart and perfectly complemented his social shortcomings.

Wealth and Morality

Two more months went by with Mark and Samantha creating and growing accustomed to new routines together at home.

One day Mark was reading on his laptop at his freshly cluttered desk in a corner of his tidy living room near the kitchen and Samantha was quietly singing while making dinner.

When she heard him stretching, she called out, "Mark, I know you don't like watching the stock market, but have you checked it the past few weeks?"

"No. Me watching it won't change anything practical. The fundamentals haven't changed… guests love the new app, reservations and market share are steadily increasing, and I still expect the stock to double within five years.

"My proposal said ten years to make it sound slightly more credible to anyone who ignored my analytical basis.

"Oh, and once I turn app maintenance over to their IT department, I'm going to have to find another job somewhere. My mind needs that…"

"I know, and I'll be happy anywhere as long as I'm with you.

"And it's too bad Colton Wingate decided against buying that company where he might've wanted you. That could've been good timing…

"But anyway, you haven't been checking PS Hospitality at all?"

"No."

"Well, I have been, and I'm excited, and I'd really like to share my excitement with you."

Mark got up and headed toward the kitchen to sit at the breakfast bar. "That's different. I know we're financially okay, so I don't care much about the market from month to month, but I care about anything you care about. What's up?"

"Your net wealth is what's up. Way up. Remember when the stock jumped up over ten percent within days of the public release of your app?"

"Yes," he replied. "You told me about it. And that triggered my stock deal for the app, even though it went down a little after that."

"Well, like you always say, the market bounces up and down, and long-term trends matter much more than minor variations… well… PSH's trend has been a slow but steady climb, and it's been above a thirty percent gain for over a month now."

"That's within the range of expectations," Mark replied.

"*Your* expectations, but no one else's.

"Well… at thirty percent, your deal is worth over sixty-five million dollars.

"And that got me to thinking… if it eventually doubles like you expect, your gain would be worth two hundred and thirty million dollars… and my one percent of that is over two million dollars! You'll have made me a multimillionaire, Mark! Me!"

"I'm glad that makes you happy."

"That's it? That's all you have to say about it?!"

Mark took a deep breath and exhaled slowly.

"No… I'm sorry. I'll try to hold up my side of a conversation. How about this…?

"You already have access to all my financial accounts so you can do anything I need done… I'd like you to ask our financial lawyer to take care of whatever needs to be done to ensure you jointly own everything in my accounts. Legally make them *our* accounts.

"I've thought of them that way ever since our first night together, but I've neglected to make it legal and permanent until now."

Samantha wiped her hands clean and sat next to Mark.

"Thank you, but I don't feel good about that. That would make me feel like a gold-digger."

"Then you need a different perspective," Mark countered.

"First, it's reasonable for you to feel that potential $2.3 million is different because you earned it. It's true that I paid you that stock, but that was part of the terms of your agreement to work for me.

"And before you try to argue your work wasn't worth that much… it was worth that much to me or I wouldn't have offered it. So… that money's special to you because you earned it.

"Second, you're not a gold-digger regarding the rest of our stock, because you're part of me. I'm not the sole individual I was before we met… I'm part of you and you're part of me.

"Does… does that explain it well enough?"

She leaned over and hugged him. "Yes, my love. I guess, sometimes it's still hard to believe you really feel that way about me."

Then she straightened up to look him in the eyes.

"Mark, you can't lie, can you?"

He furrowed his brow, then relaxed it.

"I think I probably could. But perhaps not convincingly, and I can't imagine a reason that'd motivate me to try."

"The night you first came to dinner… did I really fool you?"

"Hmm. Well, the way I think you mean, yes, you really fooled me. But that's not the way I think about it. The way I think about it is, I met Samantha that night. And fell in love with her. With you…"

Samantha hugged him tight again before giving him a kiss as she got up to check on the food.

"Mark.... how do you think of... of, uh... of Todd and Samantha. Both of them. Together, sort of. I guess I don't know how to ask what I'm trying to..."

"I might have gotten the idea. Which is interesting, because it means you've been thinking about that, so I'm glad you've brought it up, so I can share in what's going on in your mind... I'll answer in a minute, but first I'd like to know what spurred this."

"See that book on the counter? I found it while putting away things from the last box from my apartment. It's a journal my mom gave me when I was fifteen. I guess she thought it might help me to write things down, but I only did that a few days.

"Open it up and read the last three paragraphs. That's what got me thinking about Todd again."

Mark read out loud, " 'I haven't had sexual desires yet, but if I ever can, who could I have sex with? I'm not a normal male or a normal female.

"I can't have sex with a girl because my dick's way too small and permanently impotent, plus I'm sterile, but I can't have sex with a guy because I don't have a vagina, even though my body's looking more female than male now.

"I've never felt anything that sounds like what I've read or heard about how sex is supposed to feel, but could I give someone else sexual pleasure? If so, who?' "

He put the book down and thought about it, then said, "Well, you certainly have a strong desire and an excellent ability to give me sexual pleasure... but as far as Todd goes, I couldn't possibly have had sex with him.

"My brain wouldn't have let me do that. I'd have been in fight-or-flight mode if he'd tried to kiss me."

Samantha grinned at him. "Well, I sure am grateful your brain will let *me* do that. Extremely grateful. That's immensely satisfying to me."

A chime sounded from the stove.

"You ready to eat?" she asked.

"I hope I didn't upset you," Samantha said after they started eating. "You look… a little concerned."

"Oh, sorry," he said. "I was thinking about your diary entry and earlier conversation… and my mental conflict about the two of you…

"I knew Todd, and respected and admired him, and appreciated him more than I could find adequate expressions to fully describe, but I never loved Todd romantically.

"So that vague idea Todd had to appeal to me by becoming Samantha actually worked as Todd had hoped."

Samantha heaved a happy sigh. "It still amazes me that I thought of that. And that I actually tried it… but that was the best decision I ever made about anything."

Mark smiled. "And I'm extremely grateful you did. But to me, I think, Todd and Samantha are two different people.

"Maybe that's improperly projecting a split personality or something onto you, but in my mind, thinking of Todd and Samantha as the same person is kind of like trying to force two opposing magnets together, and my mind just won't let me do it.

"I liked Todd as a good friend, and I love you as my wife and my best friend."

Samantha sipped some water. "So, thinking of Todd hitching a ride in the same body as me is too confusing, and you can't reconcile that."

"I don't seem to be able to change how my brain deals with that," Mark said.

"My mind says I'm married to you, Samantha, and Todd was a treasured friend and coworker who I've lost touch with… Does that hurt your feelings?"

"No, darling. Except for the permanent reminder I encounter when I pee, I sometimes think I could forget Todd almost completely.

"I don't know if it's mentally healthy, but I, Samantha, completely own this body and mind now, so I seem to think of me similar to the way you do. It seems like my lack of testosterone made me more female than male."

"We're both strange," Mark commented. "Everyone always knew I was, and no one but you and your parents and doctors knew you were.

"Then we found each other, and you started taking care of me at work, and now you take care of me all the time."

"You take care of me, too, Mark. You make me happy and fulfilled. Life with you is better than the best dreams I ever had before I met you.

"And that would be true if we only barely had enough money for food and rent."

"Speaking of money," Mark said after swallowing a bite, "as you pointed out, if the market cap doubles as I expect, our gain will be over two hundred million dollars, so we need to start seriously working on how to give away that much wealth responsibly…

"And I think I understand how you'd prefer we go about that.

"We'll brainstorm together, you'll research our ideas, we'll refine our ideas together based on your research, we'll discuss our best options, then I'll make the final decisions, and you'll execute them for us. Yes?"

"That's perfect, Mark. Absolutely perfect."

When they finished eating and stood up, Mark walked up to Samantha before they cleared the dishes.

She turned to face him, and he wrapped his arms around her, leaned his head over as he pulled her up on her toes, and kissed her.

When they finally broke the kiss, he whispered, "I'm so happy with you, Samantha. We're two broken halves that make one perfect whole."

"That's a cliché," she giggled, "but I agree."

"Being cliché means it's so commonly said that it's boring, but many clichés are based on truth, which is why they're commonly used."

She leaned back a bit and grinned.

"I said I agree. Now, shall we start brainstorming how to choose people we can force to take a lot of our money?"

"I don't think we'll have to—"

"That was a joke, Mark."

"Ah."

* * *

A week later as they were getting up and dressed, Mark said, "Samantha, let's go to the living room and talk before we do anything else."

"Is something wrong?" she asked with a look of concern. "This isn't part of your normal routine."

"I've been getting a notion that something's bothering you, and I remembered as I was waking up.

"And as unobservant as I usually am, I'm concerned that might mean something's been bothering you a lot, and perhaps for a long time. Is that right?"

Samantha sighed. "Yes… for a few days," she said quietly, and they went to sit on the sofa.

They got settled and Mark waited until she spoke again.

"We've gotten a good start on donating to charities, but we've got a long way to go. We aren't yet giving away as much as we're making in interest and stock gains…

"Sorry, that's not what's bothering me… but our charitable giving is what's led to the… issue… that's come up in my mind…"

"Okay…" Mark acknowledged, and waited for her to go on.

"So, a lot of the charities we've been evaluating and giving to are Christian organizations… and I spend a lot of time researching them, which includes reading a lot of what's on their websites…

"And that includes the issue of life after death. And about faith in God, in addition to doing good works.

"And that led to me being concerned about morality in general… and… homosexuality, crossdressing, and feminine behavior by males in particular… and I've learned enough, and been thinking about it long enough… that it scares me…"

Mark waited again, but when it was clear she was waiting for him to respond, he did.

"Considering life after death is wise, Samantha, very wise, along with all its ramifications, and I'm very embarrassed that it's never occurred to me before.

"I guess I've been ignorantly non-religious, but now that you've brought it up, I agree that addressing eternity is worthwhile, and for us to explicitly consider morality, too. But let's deal with those concerns together, okay?"

She rested a hand on his closest thigh. "Thank you, Mark. I should have brought this up with you sooner."

Mark gazed off into space. "I've got more free time now—and I'll have too much of it soon. Once the app is fully handed off I'll need something new to occupy my brain…

"But I can start studying this some now and devote myself to it for a while after the handoff.

"After we get these personal issues settled, I'm going to need a normal job again… somewhere… doing something…

"But for now, first we need a foundation for morality, which probably involves considering one god vs multiple gods vs no god, then…

"Determine if we can either choose a moral system or discern that one's imposed on us. If one's imposed on us, we'll see how that affects us. Does that sound okay?"

"That sounds wonderful, Mark. Thank you.

"But… when we stop going to the office… we won't get our thirty minutes of cuddling on the sofa every weekday when we get home."

"Oh, no! Well, can we just set a specific time for it, close to the approximate mean time when we usually get home?"

Samantha smiled. "That would be perfect for us, I think. Six p.m.?"

Mark sighed deeply like a huge disaster had just been avoided. "Oh, yes… yes… losing that time would be… extremely disappointing."

Samantha picked up his closest hand and held it to her cheek after giving it a quick kiss. "I'm glad you like that as much as I do. And do you want to keep sex on our same schedule of every Saturday morning?"

"Is that okay with you?"

"Mark, every time I tell you that satisfying you is what satisfies me… that's not figurative, that's literal. So sex with you every Saturday morning is exactly what I want as long as that's what you want.

"But speaking of us having sex…" she continued, scooting back a bit and trying not to look worried, "off the top of your head… do you think, when we have sex… is that homosexual?

"And also, can you think of any reason why it might be bad for me to… wear dresses… and act feminine?"

"No," Mark said before pulling and lifting Samantha onto his lap so they could hug while he replied. "I've never analyzed those issues, but off the top of my head, what we do has always seemed heterosexual to me, because I'm a man, and you're a woman.

"I can see why others might disagree, but that's how it's seemed to me all along. As for you…

"I don't think you're crossdressing, and I don't think you're acting feminine, I think you are feminine.

"I think your XXY chromosomes made you more female than male, and I think you've been a lot happier as Samantha than you ever were as Todd."

"A hundred times happier," Samantha agreed. "Todd was rarely happy at all. He was just… accepting of the way things were. Stoic."

Mark noted that insight, then replied, "And you and I have been devoted to each other—faithful—no sex with anyone else.

"And I mention that because I have a vague impression that sexual promiscuity is considered immoral by most people… except those who behave that way, probably."

"I think that's right," Samantha agreed again. "But do you think we might have to change? Like stop having sex?

"Or… might I have to go back to being Todd in order to be moral?"

"I'm sorry, but I have no idea. Except if morals require that, we could consider being immoral on that issue, and take whatever the consequences would be, if any.

"And if you go back to being Todd, my brain will require that we stop having sex. But I have no foundation to base an estimation or even a guess on.

"Will… will you be able to worry less about those things as I make studying this a high priority?

"I'm completely unfamiliar with this field, so I can't estimate how long it might take for me to learn enough for us to start forming conclusions."

Samantha smiled broadly and then rested her head on his shoulder.

"I can worry a lot less, knowing my own Sherlock Holmes is on the case. And if you think we—or just I—need to change, we, or I, will do what we have to."

"Good. And I'll work on this as efficiently as I can. And—ah… and if I'm Holmes, then you're my Doctor Watson? Doesn't that mean you'll have to write a story about this?"

Samantha giggled. "Oh, no… maybe I could be the landlady… Mrs. Hudson. No… I think we'll just have to pretend Sherlock fell in love and married a woman while he was working on the Hotel App Mystery."

She waved her left hand to show off her rings.

"Sherlock and Samantha," she announced.

"Oh, I like that much better…" Mark replied. "Hey… mind if I start working on this new research right after breakfast?"

"I wouldn't dream of asking you to wait. And I'll try to be patient. I know you take a lot more time to study things than I do, especially with the pondering and analysis you do."

"I'm glad. I don't think I can change how I do things, but I think I can get us somewhere useful eventually."

* * *

At dinner a few days later, Samantha asked Mark, "Do you like your new studies so far?"

"Very much. But I thought it best to… change my strategy.

"I started out with morality as my highest priority, but then I came to realize no matter how important that is, the issue of eternal life is the most important.

"So far, that seems very complicated, but I think I've got a good approach. Do you want me to give you daily updates?"

Samantha smiled. "Only give me updates when you feel a need to share some news, or if I ask, please.

"I thought I'd be able to worry less with you working on this, and that turned out to be the case."

"Oh, good," Mark said. "I'm very glad of that. And if we can live by a moral system that gives us relevant choices, we can choose to keep things as they are.

"And it may be that our preferences will still fit within an imposed system, if that turns out to be the case."

"But eternal life comes before all that," Samantha replied.

"Yes," Mark confirmed. "And settling that issue may automatically settle many or all issues of morality."

Samantha decided to try to keep her mind on other things until Mark figured out those two big issues.

Faith

Almost two weeks later, Samantha was doing housework while Mark was at his computer as usual when she noticed from behind him that his shoulders were shaking. She paused, trying to figure out what was going on.

"Mark…? Is everything okay…?"

When he didn't reply right away, ideas like strokes and seizures popped into her mind, and she rushed to him.

"Mark! Mark, what's wrong?!"

She fell to her knees beside him as he swiveled his chair to face her, his face contorted and wet.

She grabbed his hands in hers and cried, "Mark, Honey, what is it? What's wrong, Sweetheart? Should I call an ambulance?"

Mark shook his head. "No… I'm just crying…"

"What?! Why…?! What's wrong…?!"

"In my research… I've learned things… I've realized things… and… now… some of that has changed me… somehow… and my emotions took over a couple of minutes ago…"

Samantha was shocked. Seeing her always rational source of strength shaking and crying so hard scared her to her core, but she did her best to suppress the fear and help him however she could.

"Do you think you can make it to the sofa if I help you?" she asked. "You can lie down there. Should I bring you some water?"

He started standing up. "Sofa yes. Water no."

She helped him to sit down again and get comfortable, and asked, "Do you… do you want to talk about it?"

"I need to," Mark said. "I need to talk to you about it…"

"Well, rest as long as you need to first. We have as long as you need."

"I want to start talking now, Samantha. I might have to stop, or take breaks, but I'd really like to start now…"

With his shaking gone and his crying mostly over, she began to calm down herself and decided to try to give him some physical comfort by getting on the sofa beside him with her legs tucked under her with her knees resting on his closest thigh.

That seemed to help him relax some and he wrapped an arm around her as he began to explain in his usual analytical way—except with more pauses than usual—what led up to his crisis.

He briefly explained how he evaluated religions and non-religious beliefs and how he narrowed them down to Christianity, and then focused on Jesus.

Though this new emotional side of Mark she'd never seen before was now burned into Samantha's memory, Mark had seemed to recover quickly as he spoke, to her great relief, and then she was able to pay more attention to what he was saying,

"So," Mark was summarizing, "the issue of eternal life led me to analyze the issue of God, which led me to a universe-creating single God, and that seemed likely to include a foundation for a single, imposed moral structure…

"That led me to Christianity, which led me to the things Jesus said, as recorded by four of his disciples, which include many extraordinary statements… with one statement more extraordinary than the rest, and, I think, it lies at the crux of all of Christianity—no… it lies at the crux of all of humanity…

"Jesus said, 'You must be born again.' "

"Born again?" Samantha repeated, unable to restrain herself at that. "I've heard that expression, but what in the world does it mean?"

Mark chuckled. "The guy Jesus said that to also didn't understand it. Unfortunately for me, that passage doesn't seem to have the concrete answer my mind prefers…

"But combining that part of the Bible with other parts, I think it means we're all born once from our mothers—obviously—but if we want to go to heaven for eternity, we also have to be re-born… born spiritually… And your next question is naturally how can we be born spiritually?"

Samantha nodded.

"I think that would have taken me a lot of effort, but like many things in the Bible, I'm not the first person with that question, and many others have studied it and written about it. Without going into details, backgrounds, or other explanations yet, here's my own summary…"

Mark closed his eyes in concentration.

"One… we have to have faith that Jesus is our savior. Which means we agree that we need to be forgiven because we've failed to live up to God's perfect will.

"Even if we only did one tiny thing wrong in our whole life, that means we're not spotless and we need Jesus to legally erase the bad things from our record.

"It's complicated, but that's why Jesus allowed himself to be executed on the cross, because he loves us that much—and giving up your life for someone else is the greatest love someone can have. In the terms of Judaism, he was perfect and he gave his life as a sacrifice to atone for our sins—our morally bad choices—our moral failures.

"Two... we have to repent… we have to regret the things we've done wrong and want to not do them again.

"Three… we have to accept God's Spirit into us. This is the part that confuses me the most, but I think it's like we have some kind of spiritual container inside us, but it's always been empty and will stay empty until we let God fill it up with himself—with his Spirit.

"And while it's empty, it tends to create an internal yearning for something deep within us... for a close relationship with the God who created us, and when his Spirit fills us, that yearning is satisfied.

"To the best of my understanding, that makes you born again. After that, God's Spirit sort of leads and guides us from inside, through our conscience, to live the way God wants us to, and when that means something hard, his Spirit in us gives us spiritual strength, too."

Mark slowly turned his gaze to Samantha, who had tears running down her face.

Not much louder than a whisper, she said, "I heard the phrase once, 'Jesus died for our sins,' but it didn't make much sense to me at the time, and I forgot about it.

"Now it makes sense to me, I think, because of a couple of things you said... The yearning part, and that He did that because he loves us.... Mark, do you think that's true? Do you think God loves us?"

She started crying hard, buried her face against him, and cried out, "Do you think God loves... me?"

Her tears and quivering voice caused Mark to bring her closer and stroke her hair as he murmured, "I know he does, Samantha.

"I know God loves you because Jesus sacrificed himself on the cross for you. That's the greatest proof there could be.

"And I know because I love you, and God's better at loving than I am.

"And also because... even though I don't fully understand how I know... something in me that's not my brain... something in me just knows.

"It's a certainty I didn't gain by reason and didn't confirm by understanding, but I know it. I'd stake my life on it. I think I'm in the process of staking my eternal life on it.

"God loves you, and he loves me. And I... I love Him. I love God. And like I read somewhere in the Bible, we love him because he first loved us."

Mark fell quiet and Samantha squirmed as close as she could. She wasn't sure about God's love, but she was sure of Mark's.

She remembered their first night together, and how she asked to kiss him... he accepted her request, and how powerful that kiss was—on the night that was both the best and the worst of her life.

Her thoughts then turned to the things Mark had said about being reborn. It made sense to her, and then she came up with a question.

"Mark... do you think we should do the things to be born spiritually right now? Is there any reason not to go ahead?"

Mark paused, then said, "I think Christianity is the most inexplicable religion, yet everything I've studied and reasoned have convinced me it's true. Perhaps because God is inexplicable. And now... now I realize that Jesus was both man and God. Somehow.

"The details of how that worked I don't know, but I'm convinced for multiple reasons without completely understanding it. And you probably realize better than anyone how difficult it is for me to believe something without fully understanding it."

Mark glanced at Samantha, who was paying close attention, so he went on.

"Critically, it seems clear that trying to abide by Christian rules—or any other set of rules—won't get us into heaven. We have to be born spiritually.

"And if that happens, we may experience internal changes like those many people have testified to. Those changes might include things that affect our desires, our beliefs, and our relationship."

"Our relationship?" Samantha fretted.

"I don't know yet how becoming born again may affect our morals, so I can't rule in or out what it might mean to our relationship. But I think eternal life for us is worth whatever it costs..."

Mark shifted their positions so they could more easily gaze in each other's eyes.

"Are you willing to do that, Samantha, even if it means we stop being physically intimate?"

She gazed at him with mixed emotions, then buried her face against him. "I really don't want to do that. Even if you don't mind giving that up… making you feel good that way is very important to me. Extremely important…

"And would that mean giving up hugging and kissing you? Or sleeping snuggled up to you in bed? Or… or… even me giving up Samantha?

She cried a long time, and Mark patiently waited. When she was finally almost cried out, she started thinking again—about the issue she'd raised that launched this spiritual research project of Mark's.

She was willing to go anywhere and give up anything in this life to stay with Mark. What if he went to heaven… eternity was even more important than this life. Would she give up anything to be with him there?

The answer was as painful as their first night together, when she thought she'd ruined everything. But no matter how painful, she was certain.

As if he sensed her new resolution, Mark quietly asked, "I think you're scared, but you want to do what I want, even in this. Is that right?"

Too afraid to speak at first, Samantha only nodded.

"Do you trust me to have your best and highest interests at heart in my decision?"

That she had no trouble answering.

"I do."

"Then we'll pray together and ask him to forgive us for all our sins, whatever they are, and to put His Spirit in us.

"That way, I think, we'll give ourselves to God in body, mind, and spirit, and trust God to have our best and highest interests at heart in everything he changes in us and everything he keeps the same."

"You're right, Mark. I'm scared, I'm really scared," Samantha said. "But I'm ready..."

"I am too," Mark said. "Both scared and ready. But it's the rational thing to do despite that fear. God created us. If he still wants us, despite our deep and numerous flaws, I think we'll be eternally grateful."

Samantha was breathing heavily and said, "Mark... I'm ready except for one thing, I think. I'm... I'm deeply dependent on you... I think I can only do it if you do..."

Mark tightened his shoulder-hug. "I'm ready, Samantha, so we can do it together. I'll pray out loud phrase by phrase, and you can repeat each phrase after me. Will that work for you?"

Samantha started bawling but squeaked out a yes.

They got on their knees, side by side, and Mark started.

"Heavenly Father...

"I come to you in the name of Jesus... and for any immoral choices I've made... I need your forgiveness... Please wash me clean... with the precious blood of Jesus... and make me completely yours...

"Fill me with your Holy Spirit... to give me new life... the life that only you can give...

"Renew my mind... as I read and obey your word...

"Help me grow... into the person you created me to be... and give me the ability... to live every day the way you want me to...

"I surrender all that I am to you...

"In Jesus' name, Amen."

Moments later, they gazed at each other, tears streaming down their faces, and then they hugged while they cried, still on their knees.

"Oh, Mark... Mark...!"

"Samantha...!"

"Mark... I feel different... something in me is different...!"

"Me, too!" Mark said.

Samantha quickly put a hand between her legs. "Oh..." she said with disappointment. "I thought... I thought maybe my body changed, but it didn't..."

Mark gave her a kiss, then said, "I think the immediate changes after becoming born again are typically spiritual, according to what I've learned—"

"Yeah, that makes sense. But I just felt *so* different, I thought maybe... well, whatever changes just happened, I like it... I feel lighter... and happier, and... and I'm not afraid! I'm not afraid, Mark! Of anything!

"I very much don't want our relationship to change, but I think the reason that possibility doesn't scare me now is because I trust God! God loves us, and he'll treat us as a loving heavenly father...!"

"Because that's what he is," Mark agreed.

They got up and back on the sofa, cuddling closely again, and chatted excitedly in hushed tones.

"Samantha..." Mark said at one point, "this is the biggest change we've ever had in our whole lives, and more important than everything else in our lives put together, and it's all because of you.

"Well, because of God's love, but, I mean... you're the one of us who got concerned about our eternal well-being and brought it to my attention. In addition to God, if you and I get to spend eternity in heaven with God, it's because of you..."

"Mark, you're the one of us who figured this all out. You're the one who led us in that prayer... How did you put it once? We're two broken halves who make one perfect whole?

"Maybe it was God who brought us together, even though we didn't pay any attention to him back then."

Mark replied, "That would fit with stories I've read from other Christians talking about what God has done in their lives.

"And maybe it was your XXY struggles that helped you overlook my cognitive and behavioral abnormalities enough to love me. And… I read something in the Bible like, every good and perfect gift comes from God. And you're the best gift I've ever had."

Samantha got a gleam in her eyes and said, "Stand up!" as she jumped up herself.

Surprised, Mark was slower, but he complied. "What's up? Besides us?"

"Just us…" She took a half step to put herself right in front of him, then put her hands on his chest and gazed into his eyes. "This is the way we were when I first asked you to kiss me. I just wanted to experience this moment again."

Mark slowly smiled, gazing back as his hands found her waist. "From that moment to this one," he whispered, "you're the love of my life."

Though he didn't need instructions again, Samantha whispered them anyway as she rose up on her toes.

"Lean your head down, tilt your head a little to one side, close your eyes, and let's gently press our lips together."

After a long kiss, Mark lay down on the sofa and Samantha lay on top of him, slightly off center toward the back of the sofa.

"Hey," she said, "do I work like your weight blanket when we're like this?"

"Hmm… I started having trouble going to sleep when I was… around eight years old, I think. Mom got me a weighted blanket to try and that did the trick. I've been using one ever since when I go to bed, but I never thought about how it works…"

"If it comforts you somehow, then maybe I'm comforting you with my body—and during our six p.m. sofa sessions."

"That makes sense. And I love it, if it doesn't offend you."

"It delights me, Mr. Stanford."

They fell quiet, and for a while, they just rested, savoring each other's presence and love.

A few minutes later, Samantha quietly asked, "What's next, Mark? Now that we're Christians? Now that we've been born spiritually?"

"Well... Christians usually get baptized, but I don't know much about that yet. And I think we need to exercise spiritually to stay spiritually healthy, and that means reading the Bible and praying, both of which we can do together every morning."

"Oh, I like that! Maybe curled up together here on the sofa. And could we take turns reading out loud?"

"Sure. I like that idea."

"Oh, but Mark... the questions about morality... and us... does us being born again mean you know how all that works now?"

"It means I know more than before, partly because it takes an unlimited number of possibilities and narrows it down to Christian morality, but there's still a lot about that I don't know yet."

"So you still need to study that more, too."

"Yes... but our morality shouldn't just come from my studies. From now on, our morality should be shaped at least partly by both of us, from inside, from us listening to God's Spirit within us. And that gives me an idea, Samantha...

"You have a strong dependency on me in many ways, and it just occurred to me that you might find yourself feeling dependent on God in addition to feeling dependent on me. If so, I'm sure that's a good thing, and don't worry that I'll feel bad if that happens, okay?"

"Okay, my love. That makes sense, but... I'll always need you..."

"We'll always need each other," Mark said, then thought a moment and added, "And that makes me think God will always want us to stay together and help each other."

"Oh..." Samantha said quietly, "but that doesn't mean... could it still mean I might need to stop having sex with you... Do you have any insights about that...?"

Mark thought for a moment, then said, "I don't think we need to change anything yet.

"There's still a lot I want to study and understand, but I think we can keep living as we have been unless and until God makes it clear we need to change something—either through my studies, or through speaking to our consciences, or some combination of those...

"I can share some new ideas and issues I've been thinking about along those lines, if you'd like."

Samantha looked eager. "Yes, please, Mark. I'd like that very much."

His gaze drifted up and to one side as he focused his mind. "We both enjoy sex to fill a need for intimacy. We get a lot of that from hugging and kissing, but sex adds to that in a very nice way.

"You also need sex as part of your need to serve me... Also, you've talked about a desire to be a normal woman... and with your XXY chromosomes, you have a biological basis as a contributing factor in your internal motivations and desires.

"Is your unique biology enough to make our sexual activity acceptable to God? I don't know yet, but I suspect so."

"I sure hope so!" Samantha said.

"I do, too," Mark replied. "But I only mean acceptable to God, not to other people or to our society at large. What I mean is, there may be things that God approves of that other people don't approve of.

"In fact, I'm sure there are countless issues where that's true, because many people believe contrary things about what God approves of, and sexual practices are an area where that's common.

"Another example is how a lot of people get bent out of shape over different opinions about very minor things, like tiny details about clothing."

Mark was quiet for a moment, and Samantha spoke up. "So, we really only care what God thinks about us, and not what other people think?"

"Only God will judge us when we die," Mark replied. "And no one else except your parents and doctors know your body isn't a normal female body.

"So as far as other people are concerned, we're just a normal, married heterosexual couple, and we have no obligation to reveal your chromosomal abnormalities to them."

"Good," Samantha said. "So if I understand you correctly, you think we only need to care about God's opinion about us having sex, and you think it's okay for us to continue as we've been doing, but you're not yet certain it will stay that way?"

"That's an excellent summary, Samantha. Does that uncertainty raise a fear in you again?"

"No, Mark. I'm surprised—very surprised, but I'm not afraid at all. Somehow, deep inside, I trust God. I don't know what changes may come in the future, about us having sex or anything else, but in everything… inside me somewhere, I'm relaxed and unafraid because I trust God."

Crisis

For the next week, Mark and Samantha began to adjust to their new faith, reading the Bible together every morning and ending with prayer before Mark spent the rest of the day studying and Samantha took care of everything else.

A few days into the second week, at the end of their morning prayers together, Samantha asked Mark to postpone his studying a few minutes.

Of course he agreed, and then he waited for her to get to whatever she wanted to say or ask.

"Mark, I was wondering… if you could tell me how it's going? Can you estimate yet how long it might take you to become certain if it's okay for us to have sex? Recently I've started getting anxious about it, and I don't know why. I'm afraid again…"

Then it was her turn to wait quietly.

After a few moments, Mark said, "I apologize, Samantha… you know I enjoy studying, and I've had my mind so wrapped up in it that I forgot you've been waiting for something that gives us certainty. Or as much certainty as possible. And I can give you that now.

"My only excuse for not doing it before is that it's the kind of assessment that formed slowly over time, and didn't produce a single moment of clarity…"

"That's okay, Mark. And I'm sorry if I became impatient."

"You've been very patient. Now… do you just want my conclusion, or would you also like the basis for it?"

Samantha considered it a moment and decided, "Just the conclusion."

"Okay," Mark said. "You don't have to change, and we don't have to change."

Samantha tilted her head, and her face scrunched a bit. She folded her arms and tilted her head to the other side. "Wow…"

She stood up, but just stood there a moment, before wandering to the other side of the coffee table. She stopped to look at Mark, who was watching her closely.

"Your respiration's up," Mark observed. "Is that relief or anxiety?"

"It has to be relief, right?" she said with a puzzled expression.

"My conclusion is what I was anticipating," Mark replied, "and what you were consciously hoping for, but no, it doesn't have to be relief you're feeling. And it could be a mixture of both relief and anxiety."

"But Mark… how could I be anxious now? You're right that this is exactly what I've been hoping for!"

Mark stayed seated and pondered while Samantha paced and fretted.

"Perhaps," Mark finally said, "it's what you were hoping for, but not what you expected."

Samantha froze, with furrowed brow.

"Maybe it's not," she said when Mark didn't follow up, "but I don't see how that would make me anxious."

"Whatever the reason, you're clearly very anxious now," Mark replied.

Samantha felt strange and wondered if she might cry, realizing Mark was right, and she went back to pacing, but more slowly this time.

"Maybe you need to hear the basis for my conclusion," he said.

Samantha paused again. "Okay… do you mind if I don't sit down? I'm fidgety."

"No, I don't mind… This starts with your XXY chromosomes. It also ends there, but with other major factors added.

"When your mother was about three months pregnant with you, either late in the embryonic stage or early in the fetal stage, your body reached the fork in the road for reproductive organs and started down the male path.

"However, in your case, and in some other babies with XXY and other mutations, a few days after that division began, the normal development of your male reproductive organs went awry.

"In your case, Klinefelter syndrome caused you to have severely underdeveloped testes, and much of what little testosterone they produced may have been transformed into estrogens by other organs and tissues.

"Together with the fact that you were never given testosterone therapy, it means you never—never—had normal amounts of male hormones.

"From the very early moment when your testes stopped developing, your body has always had a strongly female balance of hormones. And that means you were only a normal male for a few days."

Samantha paused in her pacing but didn't look at Mark.

"The human brain doesn't stop developing until we're about twenty-five years old," he continued, "and hormones affect that process, resulting in physical differences between male and female brains, including structural, functional, size, lateralization, and grey vs white matter balance.

"Those differences are only slight, but they exist. Your nascent reproductive organs were normal male organs for a few days but your brain has been a normal female organ for twenty-five years, and along with everything else…

"You were right when you once mentioned that maybe you should have been Samantha all along."

Samantha's mouth fell open and her shoulders dropped as she slowly turned in Mark's direction.

He waited. And waited. And she finally reacted.

"Oh my God."

She lowered to her knees and stared blankly.

"Oh my God..."

"Oh my God... Mark..."

"Samantha, when you were born, the doctors and nurses saw a tiny penis and announced you were a baby boy. There's a psychological and sociological phenomenon where people tend to stick with the first thing said or done which is known as first impression bias or the primacy effect, and that happened with the people around you.

"Every record seen by every doctor you ever went to showed you were a male, and they simply followed that path. And every one of them told you and your parents you're a boy, a male, or a man.

"They probably rarely stated that explicitly, but it was implicit in everything they said. Your parents believed you were male because they saw a baby penis when they changed your diapers and because the doctors said so. Your teachers, your friends, and everyone else believed you were male...

"Long before you knew what the difference was between boys and girls, you knew you were a boy because that's what everyone said and that's how they treated you. That's why you first believed you were a boy, and you never stopped. That's normal social development for normal boys with XY chromosomes.

"Once you started learning rudimentary biology, you learned boys have penises and girls have vaginas, so that eliminated any possibility of you questioning your basic biological sex despite your XXY Klinefelter syndrome diagnosis."

Mark paused to let her consider all that.

"But... my brain..." she muttered after a long pause.

When she stayed quiet, Mark continued.

"A brain with feminine characteristics doesn't control your masculinity or femininity, but it's a significant influence.

"Perhaps more importantly, it's not just your brain… predominantly female hormones were influencing genetic expression in every cell in your body—genetic expression with cumulative effects."

"Oh my God…"

"And not just your brain and in the rest of your physical body. Your brain developed with female characteristics, and your physical brain and the rest of your body influenced your personality and *how* you think, both logically and emotionally.

"Oh my God… oh dear God…"

Samantha slowly lifted her eyes to Mark's. "My-my whole life… is a lie… I'm twenty-five years old—that's a third of my life, Mark—I'm twenty-five years old, and my entire life so far… I've wasted the first third of my life thinking I was someone I wasn't! I was Samantha my whole life, but I didn't know it!"

Samantha stayed in that position, breathing hard but not talking. Mark got up and sat on the floor next to her, but he didn't talk either.

"I feel like I've had the stuffing kicked out of me," Samantha finally whispered. "Or like I used to have an anchor in life, and now it's gone…"

She tipped over to lean against Mark and he put an arm around her.

"It hurts," she continued. "Mentally. It seems like I ought to be happy, but…"

Mark said nothing, but kept holding her.

"Let's get on the couch," she said a minute later.

They got up, then Samantha exclaimed, "Oh, no, Mark, I'm sorry, you can start your studies now. I didn't mean to distract you this long. I don't know what I was thinking! I've got chores to do, and—"

She was interrupted by Mark pulling her into a hug, and using one hand to hold her head against him.

"Hush… this isn't the time for those things…"

She relaxed some into his hug and he guided her to the sofa. She curled up against him, and Mark patiently stroked her back.

"Who am I, Mark?" she whispered.

"You're the woman I fell in love with."

"The *woman*?"

"A woman with genetic mutations."

"Not a man with genetic mutations?"

"No. Never."

Unsure of what to say or do next when Samantha remained quiet, Mark defaulted to being analytical, but in a soft voice.

"The effects of XXY chromosomes vary between different people who have that, and that can result in testes that range from normal size to vestigial, like yours. The size of their testes usually determines how much androgens they produce, which affects everything else in their body.

"You're at the extreme end of that scale on the small side, and you've been that way your whole life…

"There are a lot of other sexual mutations, too. One of the rarest is Ovotesticular syndrome… people with that used to be called true hermaphrodites, but that term became a slur.

"They all have both ovarian and testicular tissue, and some have both ovaries and testes, and both a uterus and vagina and a penis. If they're left alone, an extreme few of them could actually impregnate themselves—but most of them aren't left alone…

"For many of them, their anomalies are obvious the moment they're born, and—according to what I read—in areas with modern medical practices, the doctors advise the parents to choose one sex.

"Then they use surgery and then hormones off and on to support them living as normal a life as possible as either male or female.

"Usually they have more male or female tissue, so the doctors recommend keeping whatever the child has the most of."

"Wow…" Samantha said. "I don't know if that would have been better or worse than… how things went with me."

"Under your circumstances," Mark replied, "I think you excelled. I can't imagine how you could have possibly done better."

She unsnuggled enough to look at him. "I don't see how you could think that…"

He replied, "You grew up with learning disabilities and under the same misapprehensions as your parents, doctors, and everyone else. Everyone believed you were male, including you, and on that basis, you graduated from high school and college with a record good enough to get a white collar job in the C-suite of a Fortune 100 company…

"Oh, yeah, you excelled, all right."

Samantha unsnuggled completely, climbed into his lap and kissed Mark passionately. "I only care that I did good enough to meet you."

Mark replied with watery eyes, "And your admiration for me in our early days… triggered feminine passion somewhere deep inside…"

He took a facial tissue from the box on the end table and wiped his eyes and nose.

"That was totally foreign and initially incomprehensible to you, and gave you an extremely difficult psychological struggle. But you not only came through the struggle, you conquered it…

"You said once that you were desperate, implying that it was desperation that drove you forward, but Samantha, lots of people become desperate and do nothing about it. You… you were brave. You were scared, but you were braver than your fear."

"I had you as a role model for bravery," Samantha said. "The way you spoke to all those executives..."

Mark smiled. "I'm very glad you found that inspiring, especially if it was critical to you introducing me to Samantha, but that wasn't bravery in that meeting. That was a lack of fear. No, what you did, for yourself, and for us, was far greater."

Samantha wiggled her arms behind his back and squeezed, then relaxed with her head on his shoulder.

"I'm amazed at your appreciation of me."

They enjoyed the hug in silence for a minute, then Mark whispered, "I thank God for you, Samantha.

"That night when you introduced yourself at your apartment... that was the real, whole you... and I loved you completely."

She nodded, then gasped and quickly leaned back to face him.

"Mark! I just remembered...! When I was a teen... I was ashamed that my voice hadn't gotten deeper like all my friends... so I started practicing speaking in a lower voice. I worked hard at it.

"I practiced every day for months... I was determined to keep it up until it became habitual, and I did... and from then on... I always spoke that way... Mark! That was my voice for so many years, I thought it was my natural voice, but it wasn't! When I started dressing up as Samantha, I noticed my voice went up, and I was glad, but... *that* was my natural voice! A female voice!

"But why did I only remember that now?"

"Psychological compartmentalization, perhaps," Mark mused. "But your high natural pitch fits with you not having a visible Adam's apple...

"And I guess dressing as Samantha overrode the habit of using an artificially lower voice."

"I'm a woman," Samantha murmured. "I was always a woman... I never pretended to be a woman... all my life I was pretending to be a man.

"I have a deformity that fooled me—that fooled everyone… but I'm a woman… and I have a husband—a loving, understanding, compassionate husband who loves me… the real me…"

"Mark and Samantha," Mark whispered. "Husband and wife."

Life is Hard

After giving Mark another bear hug, Samantha said, "If you don't mind putting off your studies a little longer—"

"No studies today," Mark said. "This is a cuddle day."

Samantha grinned and kissed him. "Cuddling, and kissing, and caressing, and everything else husbands and *wives* do."

"That includes talking," Mark replied. "You indicated there's something else on your mind."

"Yes… some things you said have made me curious… all the genetic variations that affect sexual characteristics, and us being born again now… what will happen to all that in heaven, for those of us who make it there?"

"I had a related question and looked into it some recently," Mark said, "but I only got to the point where I was sure I wouldn't find a comprehensive, detailed answer…

"Jesus raised a guy named Lazarus from the dead, and apparently people recognized him normally.

"After Jesus rose from the dead, some of his followers were able to recognize him, but others didn't. That's puzzling. That implies different people weren't seeing the same body or were seeing the same body but perceiving it differently.

"And at least some saw the wounds from when he was crucified on the cross, and at least Thomas was able to touch his body and the wounds. Yet, he could appear and disappear, in locked rooms.

"And… shortly before Jesus was executed, Peter, James, and John went with Jesus high up on a mountain and Jesus' face 'shone like the sun' and his clothes became as bright as the light, and… then they saw Jesus talking to both Moses and Elijah, who had died hundreds of years before…

"There are some other parts of the Bible that relate more to your particular situation, if you're wondering if you'll look like Todd or Samantha in heaven. Nothing definitive, but…

"Someone asked Jesus about who a person would be married to in heaven if they had more than one spouse on earth, and Jesus said in heaven people won't be married, and instead, they'll be like the angels in heaven.

"I couldn't find anything that described angel anatomy, let alone talk about sexual organs or mutations, or anything like that, so…"

Mark's voice trailed off.

"So… it's mostly a mystery?" Samantha asked with a sigh.

"As far as I've been able to determine so far, yes. Our bodies will be different, but we don't know exactly how."

Samantha got up, then knelt on the floor between Mark's knees, held his hands, and gazed up at him.

"Mark… based on things you've told me, it's clear to me how you'll answer a particular question, but emotionally, I need to hear you say it. I'm not an effeminate man, am I?"

"No, absolutely not. You're a woman with irregular sexual organs due to a genetic anomaly."

"Do you think God looks at me that way?"

"I do. I'm only human, and I don't understand God well, but on this issue, I believe he does, because I believe that's reality."

She huffed a sigh of relief, then tensed again. "So the warnings in the Bible about people having 'unnatural relations…' "

"Does not apply to you. Or to us."

After a minute of silent thinking, Samantha rested her head on his thigh and asked, "Why do some people have unnatural relations? And what does that even mean?"

"I've only given that a cursory look," Mark replied, "but it seems that expression means homosexual conduct, as opposed to a state of being. Every aspect of that whole topic is disputed by at least a few people, often arguing minutiae.

"I wouldn't be surprised if most people debating it have fixed opinions before they start their analysis, and look for confirmation of what they want the answer to be.

"As to why, there's also been a lot of debate about causes or predispositions, mostly about complex interactions of genetic, hormonal, and possibly environmental factors… but I haven't seen anyone else propose what seems like an obvious possibility to me, which is that one factor could simply be choice—at least for some people."

"Really…? But why would anyone choose that?"

"Oh, well," Mark said, "if that happens, I expect an issue like that could have countless reasons. Fear of the unknown, the primacy effect, whatever causes some young people to be rebellious, hostility toward God, belief that the opposite sex has an easier life, novelty…"

Samantha raised her head to look at him again. "Fear of the unknown? How would that work?"

"Male children have male friends and female children have female friends," Mark explained. "After puberty, it's normal to develop attraction for the opposite sex, but that can be terrifying.

"I suspect this would be rare, but if, for example, a young man knows other boys and is comfortable in those friendships, then when he develops sexual desires, if he's terrified of the unknown regarding friendships with girls, he might find it easier to explore sexuality with another boy he has an established friendship with. That might also be terrifying, though, so it might be a case of which was less terrifying."

"That's awful," Samantha said. "But yeah, I can see how that could work. I remember when my friends started dating, I thought I should. Some of my friends teased me in high school—sometimes harshly—and some of that hurt deeply.

"I thought I'd just take a girl out once or twice so my friends wouldn't wonder why I didn't, but even that simple plan was way too frightening for me to actually do it."

When she didn't continue, Mark resumed his train of thought, "And once two boys, or two girls, have any kind of sexual experience together, the primacy effect could kick in, and they just stick with same-sex behavior as the easier, more familiar path.

"That's primacy effect by choice," he continued, "but unfortunately, there's a much worse possibility where that effect might apply, and that's where virginity is taken by force, when an adult seduces, coerces, or rapes a young person of the same sex.

"That first experience is then the only thing they know, and once they have a real choice, they might find it less scary to continue with what they know."

"Wow… that's horrible!" Samantha said.

"Yes… I wonder if that's the worst evil there is. Worse than murder, because at least someone who gets murdered stops suffering. Sexual abuse is like torture where the victim's kept alive so they can keep suffering."

"Is there any way we could help… stop that… somehow?"

They thought about it for a while, then Mark suggested, "We're giving money to organizations that help widows and orphans. Helping orphans might help prevent them from falling into the kind of desperation where people take advantage of them."

"That's a great idea, Mark. That's a good start, and I have a lot more orphan-helping places on my list of possibles. I'll move them to the top of my list."

"And if you don't mind, I'll put off my other studies for now and help you with that."

"That would be wonderful, if you don't mind."

"And we can add vulnerable children to our morning prayers," Mark said.

"Definitely," Samantha replied. "Hey, one of the ones on my list helps young adults aging out of the foster care system. Without help, some of them might be vulnerable."

"Top of the list then," Mark agreed. "But we still have to make sure the places we give money to are really doing what they claim they're doing."

"And ask for God's guidance."

"I think he's giving us some of that right now."

* * *

While they were getting ready for bed that night, Samantha was thinking about her extremely eventful morning and all the things Mark had said, both about her and other people, and she came up with another question.

"Mark... have your studies included transgender people?"

"Hmm, well, that depends on how you define the term. I've been focused on biologically intersex people, like you.

"That includes people with gender dysphoria, like you, but my impression is that gender dysphoria also includes people without a biologically intersex basis for it. I've read a little about it while studying intersex issues, but I never focused on it."

"Do you suppose we could help them?" Samantha asked. "And the ones who later detransition?"

"Well, God loves everyone, and they're part of everyone. Do you have any charities on your prospect list that deal with that?"

"Not that I know of. I can look tomorrow. Support groups, maybe... but... Mark... assuming they don't have an undiagnosed intersex condition, then... if they don't have a biological cause, what does cause it?"

"Hmm..." Mark pondered. "I don't know, but for someone with gender dysphoria without a biological basis, I suspect it might be various combinations of multiple issues, like... hmm..."

Mark sat on the edge of the bed and gazed off into space. "The same issues that lead to homosexuality, maybe... and dissatisfaction with who they are seems likely... or dissatisfaction with stereotypes of their biological gender..."

"Peer pressure from friends, or online?" Samantha suggested. "Or from parents… or doctors or teachers?"

"Yes," Mark replied, "that seems plausible. Or a desire to belong to a minority group… or the excitement or appeal of following a semi-popular trend, perhaps among desperate attention-seekers…

"Oh, and the proliferation of pornography since the Internet became commercialized—that not only made it easy and free to view, it presents unusual sex practices in the most appealing ways the producers can imagine.

"That might affect anyone, but perhaps it most strongly affects those with a weak or insufficient ability to cope with stress in a healthy manner, or to distinguish between fantasy and reality…

"Hmm… a general decline in adherence to traditional culture might also be a factor for some…

"Oh, and new surgical & drug options that are highly profitable for the medical and pharmaceutical industries—which might explain why some doctors might pressure people with gender dysphoria toward transgender changes."

"Wow," Samantha said. "That's a lot of possibilities."

"Yes," Mark agreed, "and that complexity makes me wary of expanding our charitable giving focus, which would dilute our attention to needy widows, orphans, post-foster care, and intersex. That's already a lot."

"It is," Samantha said, "but how about if we make those our focus, with a secondary set of charities for individual things we come across that seem worthwhile? A miscellaneous category.

"We'd typically give them much less attention and money, but that way we wouldn't be ruling groups out just because they're not in our focus area."

"Okay. We can try that. But I want us to remain wary that we don't start spreading our attention too thin."

"Okay, thanks," Samantha said, then hesitated. "I have another question."

Mark glanced at the bed, knowing she knew he didn't like to talk after they laid down for the night, and guessed that was why she hadn't just asked the question.

"Nightcap at the kitchen table?" he asked.

Samantha hugged him. "I'll make chamomile tea."

"Why do some people insist there are only two genders?" Samantha asked as she put the water in the microwave and Mark sat at the table.

"Because they're correct, as a generalization," Mark replied. "Historically, it's very close to completely correct based on appearances."

"But generalizations aren't accurate," Samantha countered, "and appearances can be deceiving."

"Generalizations aren't *precise*, but they're often accurate as generalizations, and deceiving appearances can reinforce the generalization.

"For example, until a few months ago, everyone who saw you would've said, 'That's a man.' But now, everyone who sees you would say, 'That's a woman.' Yet you're the same person, so—"

"Oh!" Samantha interjected. "So from the perspective of anyone other than you and my parents, I appear to fit the belief that everyone is one of two genders."

"Exactly," Mark agreed.

"Hmm..." Samantha mused. "What about people who reject the idea that they're male or female?"

"Well," Mark said, "biologically—genetically—everyone is either male, female, or a combination of male and female, like you. What they feel like is a separate issue... and others can only perceive what they look like.

"But going back to the only-two-genders generalization, I suspect when people encounter folks who appear androgenous, they may instinctively try to figure out if they're male or female—I know I do for a moment before I decide to ignore the issue."

"Hmm..." Samantha said. "Why do you suppose people use that generalization?"

"Oh, that's easy. Generalizations make life easier to deal with. Most people in developed cultures these days suffer from cognitive overload, and I suspect it's a basic human instinct to simplify things...

"I suspect most people are either unaware of intersex people or they think the number of them is so small they ignore them against the simple only-two-genders idea."

He paused, then asked, "Including thumbs, how many fingers do people have, Samantha?"

"Ten. Is that a trick question?"

"It's a similar example... everyone knows that everyone has ten fingers—except... there are a very few people born with more or fewer.

"Those with more often have the extras removed. But the rule is that people have ten fingers, and exceptions are generally ignored... except by the people who are exceptions."

"Hmm..." Samantha mused again, "and... you think most people *need* simplicity in most things?"

"Yes. Different people have different social capacities, but they use up their daily cognitive energy on things they need to survive, like getting ready to go to work, doing their job, raising their children, and dealing with countless issues that are an inescapable part of their lives. So they often avoid complicated thoughts when they can."

Samantha considered that, then said, "Playing chess can be fun, but almost no working adults play it for fun as an evening's entertainment."

"That's an excellent example," Mark replied.

Then Samantha added, "So people are already stressed by life, then when they see a new headline mentioning a trans woman or something similar, it conflicts with their reassuring simplicity."

"Yes," Mark agreed. "And I expect that kind of anxiety has increased as gender dysphoria has become more common, and has broken into the news and public policy debates more often. If I understand correctly, emotional stress is a major cause of alcoholism, illegal drugs, verbal abuse, divorce, low libido, and a host of other maladies."

"My parents and I have had plenty of stress due to my XXY genes," Samantha replied, "but it never occurred to me that my condition could stress other people if they found out about me."

"I suspect many would react with compassion," Mark said, "but others wouldn't. Having their simple view disrupted might generate something like fear, anger, or hostile denial."

"I hope I never have to find out."

Mark slowly nodded as the microwave beeped.

Samantha gave a long sigh. "Life is hard."

"For everyone."

Samantha yawned as she took the water out of the microwave, and gazed at Mark.

"How about if I pour the water out and we go to bed now?" she asked.

Mark had to wait to reply until he finished a big yawn. "That sounds good. If you want, we can talk about it more when I'm not so..."

Another yawn interrupted him, and Samantha escorted him to the bedroom again.

Ever After

A few weeks later, Mark and Samantha started chatting over breakfast.

"Okay," Samantha began, "we researched what kinds of local churches are around here, came up with principles to choose one kind and chose one.

"Then we did the same for individual churches of that kind, and, theoretically, we're ready to visit one, but I kind of don't want to.

"I never realized how nervous I'd get once it was time to actually go to a church meeting."

"That surprises me," Mark replied. "You're more sociable than I am, and you've been through innumerable new social experiences as you went through high school, college, and in the corporate world.

"And you showed extraordinary courage when you became Samantha… so why is this worse than things you've done before?"

Samantha was quiet as she considered that.

Mark snapped his fingers. "You did all those things before as Todd… as Samantha, you've only worked a job you already knew from your time as Todd, and other than that, all your interactions with charities have been online or by phone. Could that be the problem?"

Samantha grimaced. "I think you're right. I— I don't know how to socialize as a woman. And I wonder… I wonder if I feel guilty because I'm hiding my XXY… situation.

"We read that Bible passage about the need for Christians to confess their sins to one another. Suppose they ask me to do that? It would be wrong to lie to them, but… I really don't want to tell anyone else about it."

"Samantha, your chromosomal mutation isn't a sin."

"Well, what is a sin? From the perspective of Christians? To the people in the church we're thinking of visiting?"

"I'm pretty sure a sin—in God's eyes—has to be something you have some control over, and you choose to exercise that control in an immoral manner.

"And if people disagree with God's opinion, what they think doesn't matter—assuming they're not in a position of power over us somehow."

"Hmm…" Samantha mused. "Maybe they won't ask about things like that… but I'm nervous they might."

Mark shook his head. "I watched a whole meeting on video and they didn't do anything like that. It was almost all singing and Robert giving a Bible speech.

"And Robert didn't say anything about sin confessions—or any other kind of confessions—when he described a normal meeting to me, but I'll text him and ask about this. I'll be subtle enough that he won't know why I'm asking."

Samantha fidgeted. "Very subtle, please."

"I'll write it, and read it to you before I send it, so I can still edit it if you don't think it's good enough."

"Thank you, Mark. But… while I think it's true that only God will judge whether we go to heaven or hell, people can be very judgmental and make us social outcasts within their group."

"Now there's something that might be a sin," Mark said, "but we chose this Church partly because these people in particular don't seem to be like that."

"That's true… that and Robert's claim to adhere to the Bible in his sermons." Samantha smiled. "Sermons, not speeches."

"A sermon is a specific type of speech," Mark countered.

Samantha sighed. "Okay, you're right on that point, but I'm still a little worried about someone finding out about me."

"If they're Christians their reaction should be compassion and understanding," Mark said. "But how would they…? If we don't volunteer the information, I'm pretty sure they don't have rituals to inspect our naked bodies."

Samantha giggled. "Okay, I think you're probably right about that, too. But suppose I'm self-conscious about what I'm hiding, and someone senses that?"

"Samantha… do you *need* to worry about something?"

"I— I don't know. I never used to be so emotional…"

"No one at this church knows anything about us," Mark said, "and all they'll learn about us is what we tell them and how they see us behave."

Samantha heaved a sigh. "Yeah… the logical part of me knows that, but the emotional part doesn't."

"That means it's stressing you. I suspect that will resolve itself if you can bear to go the first few times."

She nodded. "I hope so."

They finished breakfast, and after Samantha cleaned up as Mark shaved, they sat together on the sofa for morning Bible reading and prayer.

Before they started, though, Samantha said she wanted to continue their conversation from breakfast.

Mark waited on her as her fingers traced absent patterns on his knee until she was ready to speak.

"Mark… first I want to apologize for something… to confess something wrong I did to you…

"One day at work you wanted us to swap résumés and college transcripts, and you said something about the more we know about each other the better for making our strengths and weaknesses work together…"

She glanced away. "I should have told you then about my XXY genes… I'm sorry…"

Mark gently turned her head to face him. "You weren't expecting that, so you weren't prepared for it, and it was your deepest secret. And maybe wanting to share that secret with me was part of what motivated you to try being feminine… and ended up with me meeting Samantha.

"I think that was only a few months in between. And I'll never be able to find words adequate to describe how grateful I am for you trusting me enough to share your secret and your whole life with me."

It was a few more minutes before Samantha could voice her other question, but first, she stretched out on the sofa with her head in Mark's lap, and Mark began stroking her hair.

"Mark... even if God's views match what you've figured out about us—about me—there are so many people with other opinions about morality. Religious ones, and cultural ones… all insisting on their own rules. How do we deal with all that without it becoming a problem?"

She giggled. "Or how do I deal with that, since I don't think this will affect you?"

Mark furrowed his brow, his gaze drifting to nowhere as he organized his thoughts. "No, I think your first question is right—whatever affects one of us affects both of us.

"Human societies generate countless moral codes—normative frameworks—often rooted in tradition, fear, or social control rather than any objective foundation…

"For our own moral code, we've already narrowed our focus to what seems to be the imposed structure from being Christians, but even within that, interpretations vary wildly.

"I think we, and other Christians, have this guideline: We make decisions based on our best understanding of God's morals, and try not to offend other people if we can help it. But if it comes to a choice between God's morals and someone else's, we have to go with God's morals, even if other people punish us for it."

Samantha asked, "And we figure out God's morals based on the Bible and listening to his Spirit guiding us?"

"Yes," Mark agreed. "That's an excellent way to sum that up."

They were both quiet a minute, Mark because he was thinking, and Samantha because she recognized he was deep in thought. When he seemed to be done, she ran her fingers along his arm and smiled.

"Tell me."

Mark gazed at her and returned her smile. "I was thinking… I don't want to scare you, but… as we start to get to know other people at church… it might be good for you to look for another woman who seems friendly, and trustworthy, and compassionate, and understanding, and—"

"And could keep my secret?" Samantha finished for him. "Wouldn't it be better to just keep this between the two of us?"

Mark shook his head. "That's not what I was thinking. I was thinking that *if* you could find a woman you really like and trust… maybe you could ask her to mentor you on how to socialize.

"You wouldn't have to specify you want to learn how to do that as a woman, because she'd be certain to assume that. You could simply say you've never had much experience interacting socially with women, and now that you're a Christian, you'd like to learn."

Samantha's face lit up. "Mark! That's wonderful! That's so…"

She abandoned her search for words of thanks, climbed in his lap, and began showing her gratitude in other ways.

After their round-robin Bible reading together the next morning, they went down their wall list to guide some of their prayers.

In their rearranged living room, their sofa faced the wall that used to be behind it, and the wall was now covered with a dry-erase surface where they had a list of all the charities they were giving to.

Most of them were to help orphans and those aging out of foster care, plus a few for poor, isolated widows, and support groups for people with XXY and other intersex genetic anomalies, and a few outside those groups.

After their prayers that morning, Samantha commented, "Boy, the charity rating agencies sure have helped us avoid some bad charities so we can use our money wisely.

"That and your policy of us only giving amounts that fit with what they're already handling. No huge gifts to charities with only a history of small budgets until they can grow into it."

"Speaking of which," Mark said, "the charity you found that helps people come out of prostitution... they could do a lot more but they don't have good enough management, so this week I'm going to see if I can get the managers of our biggest orphanage group to help the ex-prostitution group get organized and trained—with us paying all the costs for that."

"Oh, Mark! That's great! If that works, maybe we could do more of that to help some of the smaller groups get bigger and wiser."

"Oh, I hadn't thought of that. Great idea, Samantha!"

* * *

"Samantha... Samantha..." Mark prodded her awake in the middle of the night a few days later.

"Yes...? What is it, Mark...?"

"I have an idea and I need you to take notes, otherwise I'll never remember it in the morning."

She paused, then pushed herself up, disappointed... a little at being woken from sound sleep, but mostly because it wasn't what she'd always dreamed of being woken up for ever since they got married.

She turned to put her feet over the edge of the bed and reached for her phone while she struggled to open her eyes. Once it was open to her quick-notes app and she could see it, she said, "Okay, Mark, I'm ready..."

Mark was still lying face up. He paused, then said, "I want to write an app for free for people with sex-related chromosomal anomalies, and their families and friends. It'll be completely free for users, and authentication will be available to help filter out predators, but optional.

"I'll make it so support groups can each have their own private-label instance, and have a members-only area… I had more ideas, but that's all I can remember right now. Maybe when I read that tomorrow it will help me remember or rethink what I've already forgotten…"

Mark was patient and quiet, knowing Samantha needed time to turn things he said into good notes.

"Okay," Samantha said a few minutes later. "Want me to read it back now?"

"No, thank you. Let's go back to sleep."

Samantha paused, then turned her phone off, and set it back on the side table, but she didn't lay down right away.

"Something wrong?" Mark asked. "Oh… I guess I should've gone to my desk to make my own notes and not wake you. I'm sorry. I guess I'm just in the habit of you taking notes for me."

She didn't reply right away, then turned toward him. "Mark… you can wake me up anytime for anything, and I love taking notes for you, so that's not what's bothering me…"

With a lump in her throat, she added, "On our first night in bed together, I promised you that you could wake me up at any hour of the night for sex, and you said that was an extraordinary offer, and you thanked me…"

"I remember that…"

"But you've never taken me up on that…"

Mark was quiet a moment, then said, "And you've been wanting me to?"

Then it was Samantha who was quiet again before admitting, "Yes…"

Mark rested a hand on her knee, then asked, "Would now fulfill that longing for you?"

"Yes..."

When they were done, they finally lay down to sleep again and Samantha snuggled into him, warm and very content, and her mind wandered and savored many of their intimate moments and many of the precious things Mark had said to her since their first night together.

Finally, she started drifting off back to sleep again. But then she thought of something and realized she needed to write it down, or she'd forget it.

She really, really didn't want to get up again... but it was for Mark... and it might be important to other people.

So she worked at unsnuggling from Mark without waking him and succeeded, then she got her phone again. She found the notes she'd just taken and added, "Users need to be able to share their birthdays if they want to. And any other special days."

She turned it off, put it down, resnuggled, and was sound asleep in moments.

* * *

"What are you doing?" Mark asked one Saturday after they'd been going to church for about a month.

"Getting ready for when we get baptized tomorrow," Samantha replied. "When I thought I was Todd, I used a compression band to camouflage my breasts. Now I'm trying to make something similar to make absolutely sure no one can see a tiny bulge between my legs after I get dunked and come up out of the water.

"I bought something for that, but I wasn't happy with it, so I'm trying to make my own."

Mark raised an eyebrow. "Huh. Okay, but—"

"After I finish sewing this, I'm going to wear it while I sit down in our bathtub, and when I get up, you're going to see if it works. And I'll change it until it works *perfectly*."

Mark smiled. "Okay. But after that, let's get a shower together."

"What? But this morning we already... oh, okay, Honey."

After their shower and drying off, they lay down on their bed to rest, and Samantha snuggled close.

"Any regrets about marrying me?" Samantha asked.

"Just one where I wish we'd grown up together and gotten married as soon as you were old enough."

"Mm... hey..."

"Yes?" Mark prompted.

"Change of topic. You've started working on a charity app, so you've put off looking for a normal job a little longer."

"Yes..."

"And you're making it customizable so each charity can put their own branding on it... and we've started helping some small charities start getting better organized...

"What if you put that all together? What if you make a full time job out of this app? Could you modify it so that it not only works for charities, but for any groups that are membership based?

"Charities get it for free, but everyone else has to pay? And for the little charities who can't even figure out how to do the custom branding, we could do that for them, too, and could you create a management training program—accessed through the app?"

Mark grinned as he shifted so they were facing each other. "You're a genius!"

Samantha blushed. "You're the genius, but I'll take the compliment as a sign that you're rubbing off on me."

Mark gave her a quick kiss.

"Expanding my app to commercial membership groups will be very easy—programming-wise—and I like all the rest of your proposal, but it would mean creating a legal business entity, with marketing, technical support, liability insurance, and all the rest...

"We'd either have to hire people to help us, or... I think we could find a company that would take us on as sort of a subsidiary, where I provide the coding, and they handle all the business management. That way we might be able to prevent it from interfering with our home life."

Then Mark tilted his head. "Unless you want to be the CEO and take all that on."

"Oh, no!" Samantha said. "I like our home life just like it is, so your idea sounds great. Maybe you could ask Colton Wingate if he has a company this would fit into."

"If he's not too demanding," Mark said, "but it won't hurt to ask. And if he doesn't, he might know someone else who does."

* * *

A few days later, they woke up a little early and Samantha snuggled close.

"Mark…?"

"Hmm…?"

"I've been thinking about the possibility of us adopting a child…"

"Oh?"

"Maybe an unwanted child that has mixed up genes…"

"I've been thinking about that, too," Mark replied. "But before you ask why I didn't mention it, it's because I didn't want to put that idea in your mind. I thought it was important for you to come up with that idea yourself."

She kissed his chest. "Thank you, Mark, my dear, extremely considerate husband. Hearing you say that out loud… I think you were right. I needed to get there on my own. But… are you okay with being a father?"

"I have no illusions about that, Samantha. My traits will make me a very poor father, but with you as their mother and primary caregiver, I think you'll adequately compensate for my shortcomings."

She shook her head. "I think you have more empathy and considerateness than anyone else I know, and I think you'll be a great father."

"Well… I guess we'll find out," Mark said. "I've looked into adoption some, and it appears it can take a very long time and be very frustrating… however, if we're willing to take a baby no one else wants… that might make part of the process easier. And by the way, no baby could be more fortunate than to have you as their mother."

Samantha unsnuggled enough to then dig her arms under him and she hugged him as tight as she could, long and hard.

When she finally let go, Mark said, "I was also thinking we could start looking for somewhere else to live.

"Somewhere better suited for children, like a small town… like… near your parents… who might like to have grandchildren nearby."

Samantha squealed, then thanked him in between smothering him with kisses.

* * *

Several months later, it was Samantha who snapped wide awake and sat up with a sharp gasp. "Oh! Oh…! Mark… Mark…!"

He slowly came to, then became alarmed and came fully to his senses. Before he could speak, as soon as Samantha thought he was awake enough, she started talking rapidly.

"Mark, I just woke up from a dream—except it wasn't like a dream—I don't know what it was like, but…

"Maybe it was like I was in heaven—like *we* were in heaven—you and I… and… it didn't look like a *place* of any kind… but there were lots of people around us, and… things… crazy-looking… things—living things… and people there knew us, and everyone was happy, and some of the people were from our church, and oh! Mark!

"There were people coming up to us, and some of them recognized us even though they never met us or saw pictures of us, but they knew us… and Mark… there were so many of them… hundreds of people who became born again through the charities we helped financially… and they were thanking us, and hugging us! Oh! And Mark…!

Samantha started crying and struggled to get the words out.

"Mark… everyone knew me as Samantha—as Samantha, Mark!"

Then Samantha was crying too hard to talk anymore, and Mark shifted around to hug her better.

When she started calming down some, they started chatting and talked a long time, with Samantha describing other things she'd seen, and Mark asking questions.

"The things you said about not seeing anything like a building or earthly scenery…" Mark commented after a while, "that fits something that I've been thinking a lot about off and on lately."

"Oh? Tell me!"

"Well, Jesus was praying… the night before he was executed, I think… and part of his prayer was, 'Now this is eternal life: that they know you, the only true God, and Jesus Christ, whom you have sent.' "

"I remember that verse!"

"Well… I guess I had always thought that eternal life meant never-ending-existence in a place called heaven, and maybe it includes that… but Jesus' prayer defines eternal life as knowing God.

"Not a place, not a duration, but… knowing God. And after being born spiritually… that makes sense to me—at least a little bit."

"Wow…" Samantha enthused. "God sure has changed us, and given us so much, but the most important thing he's given us isn't a thing… it's Himself!"

"Yes…" Mark agreed, "and it's awesome. *He's* awesome."

"And Mark… all our unusual traits that we've always felt were… unfortunate… they aren't a curse—they've been central to our purpose in life. To God's purpose in our lives."

Mark kissed her tenderly, then whispered, "I said once that we're two broken halves that make one perfect whole, but now I think I wasn't looking at that from God's perspective.

"I think maybe we aren't broken, we're just unusual… and that God made us for each other, to take what's unusual about us and use it to make the world a little bit better."

Samantha nodded while hugging him tight, and she prayed out loud, "And thank you, heavenly Father, for giving Mark and me to each other."

End

Notes from the Author

Thank you for reading this first book in the Intersections Romance series.

Finding great romance can be difficult for anyone, but it can be especially challenging for people navigating issues like intersex conditions, gender dysphoria, or Autism Spectrum Disorder—experiences that are often misunderstood or overlooked.

These themes of neurodivergence and other biological variation resonated with me as I explored how they shape personality, relationships, and belonging.

Though I may not be intersex myself, I approached this story with care, drawing on thorough research and a desire to portray these realities respectfully and realistically, and I'm grateful for the insights the process brought me.

I chose these protagonists because potential romance complicated by sex development variation and neurodivergence offer a compelling lens for examining intimacy, acceptance, and love. Then the research became unexpectedly personal and enriched the story in ways I hadn't anticipated.

CROSSOVER

Divergent is a contemporary romance and doubles as psychological literary fiction—deeply immersing readers in the characters' inner lives and the forces that shape them.

Yet the most striking genre crossover is the open pairing of natural sexuality and lived Christian faith—two topics rarely seen together in the same story.

Sexuality is portrayed with candor and sensitivity, reflecting its essential role in the protagonists' growth, including one brief, non-explicit intimate scene.

Faith is woven throughout because it's also essential to both characters' lives—as it is to mine—and inseparable from their questions about love, morality, and grace.

Together these elements aim to illuminate some of the real challenges faced by people with ASD Level 1 and intersex conditions—portrayed, I hope, with care and realism.

THEMATIC SEQUELS

Every person is unique, but differences are often magnified in people who are biologically or socially divergent in some way. Some blend easily into society; others struggle or clash.

Each divergent-related condition can produce a wide array of unique traits, offering rich possibilities for romance stories. *Divergent* is the first in a thematic series exploring different forms of human divergence. Next is *Chrysalis*, featuring a character who discovers they have an ovotesticular condition, followed by *Toast, Resonance,* and more in development.

RESOURCES

If you want to learn more information about being intersex, or need support, interACT can be found online at www. interactadvocates.org, and they maintain lists of support organizations around the world. They also offer a free 3-page Patient Self-Advocacy Toolkit to support communication between intersex people and healthcare providers.

They also offer a free 3-page Patient Self-Advocacy Toolkit to support communication between intersex people and healthcare providers, especially concerning needs that many providers are not yet trained to recognize.

GRATITUDE

I'm deeply thankful to my wife Carla for her lifelong support in all my endeavors, to friends who encouraged my poetry collection *Crimson Leaves: Poetry Celebrating Romance*, and to the team at Wipf and Stock for being willing to publish a novel that's very divergent from normal fare.

BELOVED READERS

These characters and this story are close to my heart—but not nearly as close as you, the reader who has journeyed with them to the end.

Fictional worlds only fully come alive in the minds of dreamers, writers, and readers, and each of you imagines my characters a little differently. Thank you for giving them that life, and for spending time in their world.

Whatever you felt—joy, reflection, connection, or even disagreement—I'm truly grateful.

Warmly,

John Donovan Lambert

About the Author

John D. Lambert

Eclectic Eccentric

Curator/Editor/Poet of
Crimson Leaves: Poetry Celebrating Romance

John and his wife Carla have been very happily married for over 40 years, with four grown children, and he was fortunate to have parents who were excellent role models and who themselves were very happily married for 37 years until parted by death.

John has multiple degrees, including history, literature in English, psychology, and sociology, which are relevant to the study of romance to greater or lesser extents, but he's spent more time independently studying romance than for all his degrees combined, in order to help him become the best husband he can be.

While studying romance in his spare time, John had a long career in I.T., but an attack of viral encephalitis knocked him into early retirement.

In the years following encephalitis, recovery has been steady but very slow, and most successful in fiction and poetic writing skills, plus the research skills necessary for writing.

In 2023 he brought back into print one of the first romance novels ever published in English, *Lindamira*, and in 2025 self-published the extensive love poetry anthology *Crimson Leaves: Poetry Celebrating Romance*, which was a finalist in the 2025 Readers' Favorite Awards.

John hopes his stories of overcoming and enduring love inspire readers as much as real-life romance has inspired him.

Additional biographical information:
www.JohnDonovanLambert.com

Chrysalis

Book 2 of the Intersections Romance Series

Coming Soon
Pre-Order on Amazon

A jaded young man in a dead-end job submits his photo to a talent app, and is shocked when it reveals his intersex potential for stunning femininity. That alone is more than enough to grapple with... but then questions of romance begin to emerge.

5-STAR REVIEWS FROM READERS' FAVORITES:

"Readers interested in personal identity stories, especially those involving intersex experiences, will find this book meaningful and fascinating. Very highly recommended." –Makeda Cummings

"The plot flows seamlessly, leaving no room for confusion, and the amazing narration also adds to the overall beauty of the work." –Frank Mutuma

"*Chrysalis* is an insightful book and a must-read for anyone who wishes to learn about the challenges that intersex people face and how beautiful their lives can be." –Doreen Chombu

Preview of *Chrysalis*

Manhattan Talent

Henry and Mike were laughing like hyenas in the breakroom when I trudged in, and Henry said, "Leo! You oughta do this!"

Mike kept laughing as Henry toned it down a notch to talk to me. "Seriously, Leo, you're the best looking guy here! If any of us have a shot at using this to get out of here, it's you!"

I wasn't interested in being the butt of a joke, but the idea of getting out of telephone technical support hooked me. "Yeah?"

"Yeah, yeah!" he said, showing me his phone. "This company's looking for models, men and women. All you have to be is good looking. High pay, all training provided, no experience necessary!

"They're trying to crowdsource auditions to find new talent, and all you have to do is download their app, submit your photo, and boom—the app tells you if they might be interested in you."

In between bouts of laughter, Mike said, "Henry tried it, and it was an instant rejection!"

"Their loss," Henry confirmed with a grin.

They teased me some more while yakking and laughing but their break was over so they had to quit.

"It's Manhattan Talent," Henry said on his way out. "Seriously, you should try it!"

I got a cup of black coffee and sat down with my back to a wall, as usual, so no one could see my phone over my shoulder.

I sighed deeply and tried to relax my shoulders as I turned my phone on while wishing once again that we were allowed to play handheld game machines while on break.

With no one else on break and nothing more important to browse, I did a search for Manhattan Talent and looked for third-party info first.

I didn't see any scam reports and only good reviews. They're a private modeling and talent agency, known mostly for their fashion industry work, located here in New York City, which makes sense for a talent agency, I guessed.

So I went to their website, which looked legit, and it made it clear all auditions had to start with their app, but it mentioned you could download the app and audition both for free and anonymously. Which also made sense, because I doubted Henry would've paid to do that.

I downloaded the app, opened it, and it hyped what a great opportunity they were offering and how easy it was to audition.

Fashion, acting, and other opportunities… high pay, international travel possible, all expenses paid, no experience required, all training provided… oh, and this was important, "Manhattan Talent will never ask you for money. Never. Not for fees, not for headshots, not for anything."

To audition… take a photo of your face from the front and from the side. Hair doesn't matter as long as it doesn't cover the face or ears. Age… Height… Weight… Oh, interesting… "Sex: Male, Female, or Intersex. Huh."

"The Manhattan Talent system will promptly tell you if you have a look that we're looking for. Additional information provided to those who pass this audition."

I set my phone face down and thought about it as I continued to nurse my coffee. High pay, no experience required.

They probably get thousands of people doing this, and the more people auditioning, the lower the chances of any one person, like me. And if their system was decent, they should be able to handle millions of auditions. But… auditioning was easy, free, and anonymous…

My phone had the app open, and it'd only take a few seconds to snap a couple of pictures… but if someone came into the breakroom right at that moment… nope, nope, nope.

A few hours later I got home to the tiny apartment where I rented a tiny room. No one else was home, and I fixed myself something to eat and enjoyed it in peace for once.

After cleaning up after myself, I went to my room, closed the door, propped up on my pillows on the bed and got my phone out to while away some time.

After keying in my security login PIN, my phone opened to the Manhattan Talent app, which I'd forgotten about. I started to close it, but changed my mind, and figured I'd waste a minute or two to try it.

Twenty-two years old, five foot seven, 125 pounds, male, photo from the front… photo from the side… and… submit.

"Congratulations! You're one of the very few who pass the Manhattan Talent photo audition!"

Huh. I'd be thinking scam, but Henry got rejected… Well, now what do they say…

Next step is… oh, I have to drop the anonymity and schedule an interview. I guess that makes sense. Name, address, phone…

Hey! They'll pay me a hundred bucks for completing the enrollment info, another hundred for doing the interview, and five hundred if I pass the interview! Dang!

Let's see… payment methods… yeah, they include one I already use, and even offer a crypto option… that's cool—or would be if I set up a crypto wallet.

I put my personal information in and moments later got a notification on my money app. A hundred bucks. For nothing. That was… impressive, somehow.

And two notifications in the app… one about the payment… oh, wow, and they say since I live in New York City they'll send a limo to take me to my interview! Me? In a limo?!

And I can schedule a two-hour interview any weekday, from 10 a.m. to 2 p.m. Since Thursday's my usual day off, I won't have to miss work…

But no more info about the whole deal. I guess that will come after the interview, if I pass. I wonder what the pass/fail rate is for these interviews?

The interview schedule had an opening on my next day off in three days—this Thursday, at 10, so I took that, and a minute later a notification said the limo would pick me up at 9 a.m.

I had a hundred questions, but there wasn't any other interesting information in the app, and there wasn't a way to contact them.

I searched the Internet, and found tons about the company, but the only posts I found about this auditioning process were from people who didn't pass it… and the only contact info I could find was their street address and phone numbers for some very business sounding offices.

With nothing else to learn until the interview, I put my phone down on my bed and thought all this over.

It was exciting… it might mean a much more enjoyable and much better paying job… but it'd be better not to get my hopes up yet. Try to hold that off at least until I saw how the interview went.

After a while, I went back to my usual evening activities of doom scrolling on my old, cheap Android phone with a cracked screen and playing my one luxury—my treasured handheld game machine.

Except all this Manhattan Talent business kept distracting me.

Should I tell anyone about this? If I tell my roommates or coworkers, they might tease me if I don't pass the interview…

Come to think of it, they'd probably start teasing me immediately.

Except Henry. And I only started this because he urged me to. But if I told him, would he blab it to others? Better to wait and see what happened after the interview.

What would happen after the interview? If I didn't pass, nothing, I guess. Just something else to try to forget.

And if I pass? Manhattan Talant lists fashion, movies, TV, and theater as their areas. They wouldn't want a guy for fashion—I don't think—and the others are all acting.

So… if I pass… they might start training me to become an actor?

Was I good-looking enough for that? Well, I passed the first photo-based audition, so… maybe? But probably not as a leading man, because those tend to be tall, with very few exceptions.

Supporting actor… I wonder how much that paid? Not the biggest bucks, but more than tech support?

Hmm… maybe I'd have to keep doing tech support and do acting on the side?

That thought was a huge let-down.

Well, they already paid me a hundred bucks, and I'd get at least another hundred. And if I passed this interview, another five hundred, even if I never did anything else.

Seven hundred total, for nothing!

I never had much growing up, and ever since I got a job, I'd been scrimping and living as cheaply as possible to save every penny I could, and so far I only had a little over twelve hundred bucks. Seven hundred was two or three years' worth of painful saving.

I went to the bathroom and studied my face in the mirror. Same old face… but a new realization.

Maybe I was "good" looking—Henry genuinely seemed to think so, but I certainly wasn't rugged-looking. What kind of characters would someone with my face play?

I couldn't come up with an answer for that, but maybe I'd find out in the interview.

Sleep didn't come easily that night, which made working the next day even worse than usual.

And the trip home from work the next day was weird. I was excited, but trying not to be. One more day of work, and then my interview. And the limo ride!

That evening was worse than the first one. Lots more questions, and not a single answer.

For the second night in a row, I didn't sleep well, and the next day at work was hell.

On the way home, my mind was kind of numb from lack of sleep, but at least my interview was the next morning.

Except… if I couldn't sleep again, I'd be a zombie and fail.

To my surprise, I went to sleep quickly that night, and slept well. Due to exhaustion, I guess, but at least the timing was good.

I even woke up happy, which almost never happened. Probably because I was about to ride in a limo and get paid a hundred dollars for showing up.

Even if I failed the interview completely, I'd still be two hundred dollars better off than I'd been before Henry urged me to check this out.

www.ingramcontent.com/pod-product-compliance
Lightning Source LLC
LaVergne TN
LVHW020638100826
845148LV00012B/2240